T0163847

STRANDED at Romson's Lodge

STRANDED
at Romson's Lodge

J. L. Callison

New York

STRANDED at Romson's Lodge

Published in New York, New York, by Morgan James Publishing. Morgan James and The Entrepreneurial Publisher are trademarks of Morgan James, LLC. www.MorganJamesPublishing.com

The Morgan James Speakers Group can bring authors to your live event. For more information or to book an event visit The Morgan James Speakers Group at www.TheMorganJamesSpeakersGroup.com.

Shelfie

A **free** eBook edition is available with the purchase of this print book.

CLEARLY PRINT YOUR NAME ABOVE IN UPPER CASE

Instructions to claim your free eBook edition:
1. Download the Shelfie app for Android or iOS
2. Write your name in **UPPER CASE** above
3. Use the Shelfie app to submit a photo
4. Download your eBook to any device

ISBN 978-1-63047-736-3 paperback
ISBN 978-1-63047-737-0 eBook
Library of Congress Control Number:
2015913378

Cover Design by:
Kurt Schoenfielder

In an effort to support local communities and raise awareness and funds, Morgan James Publishing donates a percentage of all book sales for the life of each book to Habitat for Humanity Peninsula and Greater Williamsburg.

Get involved today, visit
www.MorganJamesBuilds.com

Habitat
for Humanity®
Peninsula and
Greater Williamsburg
Building Partner

DEDICATION

To the memory of my father, Robert William Callison,
who did not live to see this book completed,
but encouraged me to write it.
September 1931 to December 2013

To my mother, Bertie Lou Perry Callison,
the best mother I ever had, and she is a good one.

And

To my wife, Linda, who has stuck with me for thirty-eight years.

PREFACE

When reading this story and the actions described, please understand the author does not condone all activities as written. The author attempted to write based on life as commonly lived rather than how it ought to be lived. It is incumbent on readers to determine proper action or lifestyle based on their own beliefs and convictions. Each of us must "write" our own life story so that when we stand before God, we do so without shame, resting in the forgiveness we receive through Jesus Christ, in order to hear "Well done, my good and faithful servant." Therefore, some of the actions or activities portrayed may not agree with your beliefs or standards. It is hoped this story will help you determine what your convictions are and ought to be, not based on what you read here, but based on what you read in the only authority that really counts, the Bible.

ACKNOWLEDGMENTS
With Gratitude

Sgt. Joe Sprecco (Retired); San Diego County Sheriff Department, CA
Sgt. Bill Rygh, Jr.; Oak Park Police Department, IL

These men advised me on the police procedures described in this book. Without their guidance, I would have made obvious my lack of knowledge. Thank you, gentlemen!

Mr. Russ Martin; Wipaire, Inc.

Mr. Martin was gracious enough to spend time with me on the telephone, helping me understand some of the modifications to the De Havilland Beaver described in this story. He knew he had nothing financial to gain from giving me his time but was gracious and helpful. I am in his debt.

Dr. Mike Enderby

Mike Enderby was kind enough to proofread my tale when first written, and he provided valuable insights into the story. I am most appreciative of his help and friendship.

Mrs. Teresa Carrillo

Teresa Carillo edited my story concept and gave more than a little guidance to this fledgling author, who didn't know what he was doing but had a story he wanted to tell. Teresa is the one who made it readable.

J.P. Summers; Author

Without her help, encouragement, and advice, this book would still be in the dream stage. J.P.—a chronic migraine and cluster headache sufferer—encouraged me to continue even through my cluster headache attacks. I appreciate her advocacy for more research into our little understood, and often overlooked, maladies. Thank you!

Mr. Kurt Shoenfielder

Kurt, owner of Throttle5 Creative Solutions, designed my book cover. I appreciate his excellent taste and ability to take my story concept and make it visual on the first try. Thank you, Kurt!

Robin LaLena; RN

Robin gave medical insight into the story and guided my descriptions of Charles Sitton's care. Thank you!

Linda C. Callison

I am grateful for Linda's knowledge of grammar and willingness to copyedit this book. It was an unsung task but most necessary.

Michelle Harper

Last, but certainly not least, Michelle did a final edit and gave guidance to improve the way I told the story. I'm grateful for her assistance.

CHAPTER 1

Elizabeth Sitton wept silently with her eyes closed. She didn't know where they were going, and she didn't care. She wanted to go home. Jed Romson knew where they were going. Knowing, though, made things no better. His back was stiff from sitting hunched over with his hand cuffed to Elizabeth's through the seat supports.

Jed looked at the back of Pete Richardson's head. Pete, Romson Industries' company pilot, flew the company aircraft, a De Havilland Beaver, a superb plane for getting in and out of remote areas. Jed knew the Beaver's capabilities would be needed to land on the lake by the company's hunting and research lodge.

Great, Jed thought. *Fifty miles of wilderness to any town, I'm stuck with a girl who knows nothing useful, and I have no idea where to find a hunting camp. Thirty-five miles? I don't know. I just don't know.*

CHAPTER 2

April 28, 1985, had started off well enough. Jed and Elizabeth, both seniors, returned from their senior trip after an all-night flight. It had been a great ten days in Germany, Switzerland, Liechtenstein, and Italy. Both were glad, though, to be home.

While the guys were unloading the luggage, Mrs. Dewitt, the school secretary, called out to Jed. "Mr. Sitton called. Could you drop Elizabeth off on your way home? He's sorry, but he got called in to the plant because of a breakdown."

"Sure, no problem." Jed grabbed Elizabeth's bags, threw them into the back of his Bronco, and opened the passenger door. He passed her house on the way to his own anyway, and he knew his folks weren't home. He helped her into the passenger seat of his Bronco, closed the door, then went around and got into the driver's side and started the engine.

Elizabeth pouted. Her dad always got called in. He didn't think the factory could run without him! To a measure, it couldn't, but that didn't make Elizabeth like it any better. Since her mother died of cancer three years ago, it was just the two of them, and Elizabeth had missed her dad terribly while she was in Europe.

Meanwhile, Pete Richardson timed his abduction just right. He parked in the driveway of an empty house a block from the school and waited for the bus to arrive from the airport. When he saw the bus was unloaded, he drove his car to a spot just short of the school drive and turned the engine off. He released the hood latch and got out of the car, but he didn't bother pulling the key; he wouldn't need this car any longer.

Opening the hood, Pete bent over the engine as if looking for a problem while he kept one eye on the school parking lot, watching for Jed's Bronco to pull out. He rubbed his hands on the top of the engine just enough to get some dirt and oil on them and smudged more dirt on his forehead, as if he had brushed the back of his hand across it. When he saw Jed's Ford Bronco move, he stood with hands on his hips looking disgustedly at the car. Pete knew Jed would stop, and Pete could take over from there.

Seeing Pete standing by his car, Jed stopped his truck and rolled down his window. "Hey Pete, what's wrong?"

"Oh! Hi, Jed, glad to see you! My engine isn't running, and I have to get to the hangar right away for your dad."

Jed turned to Elizabeth and asked, "Are you in a big hurry? Would you mind if I dropped Pete off at the plane on the way home?"

Elizabeth looked at him with a frown and said, "It really doesn't matter. I've no reason to hurry home. There's no telling when Daddy will get there."

Jed turned back to Pete and said, "Jump in the back seat if you want. I'll be happy to run you out to the plane."

Pete grabbed a bag from the back seat of his car and walked over to the Bronco and crawled into the back seat. "I'm sorry. I didn't know you had your girlfriend with you." This extra girl would change his plans quite a bit, but it actually might work better.

"Oh, Elizabeth isn't my girlfriend. She's Mr. Sitton's daughter. I'm just giving her a lift home because her dad is stuck working on a breakdown out at the plant."

Jed drove to the company hangar, which was between Hoppleberg's small airport and the lake. . "Here you go, Pete," he said as he turned around to look at Pete, but his eyes bugged when he saw the .38 caliber revolver Pete held in his hand.

"I'm sorry, Jed, but I have to do this. I have no other choice. You won't be hurt—I promise you, but I have to be sure of things. Now, I need you to drive the Bronco into the hangar."

Jed parked the Bronco inside the hangar next to the airplane. At Pete's order, he unloaded and secured their luggage in the back of the airplane and then climbed into the back left seat. Elizabeth sat down in the seat next to him. Pete handed her a handcuff and told her to put one end of the cuffs around Jed's right wrist, then pull it through the seat support and fasten the other end around her own left wrist. He watched carefully as she did so, slipped the gun into his pocket, pre-flighted the airplane, pushed it out of the hangar, and closed and locked the doors. Pete confirmed the door was latched and from his pocket pulled a small tube and removed the cap. He inserted the tip of the tube into the keyhole, squirted a small amount of liquid into the lock, capped the tube, and tossed it into the lake. He climbed into the pilot's seat, started the engine, and took flight.

CHAPTER 3

Hours later, Jed looked out his window when the plane banked to the left and started to descend. Sure enough, there was the company's testing lodge and the lake below. Shortly after James Romson, Jed's father, started Romson Industries, he recognized the need for a remote location with severe weather conditions to test cold weather gear and equipment. This lodge, an old lumber camp, fit the bill perfectly. Romson Industries owned over one hundred thousand acres in the most remote area of the continental United States, with less than one person per hundred square miles. Jed knew his chances of walking out to safety were nil, especially since he had to babysit a tenderfoot girl.

Pete turned his head and reached behind the seat with a set of headphones and shoved them at Jed. Jed struggled to put them on with his left hand and managed to do so on the third try. He pulled the microphone down in front of his lips.

"Can you hear me, Jed?"

"I hear you."

"Look, I'm really sorry I had to do this to you. I'm in a tight spot, and I don't have many options. Listen carefully to what I have to say, and you will be okay."

"I'm listening," Jed said, but the sarcasm was lost on Pete.

"Here's the deal. I stocked the lodge for the company's plant managers' fishing trip. You will have plenty of food, and it is not all that cold, except at night. Plenty of firewood is cut and ready. I hadn't planned on you being with a girl, but that can't be helped. I can't really take her back now, can I?" He chuckled, then continued. "I think she will actually make it easier for me to get your dad to come up with the money. In fact, I might just up the price.

"I wanted to leave you where I knew you would be safe. The last thing I want is for you to be hurt. I'll be down in the Cayman Islands about this time tomorrow evening, and I'll message him from there and give him the idea you are down there with me. Besides, without the plane, he won't be coming up here to look now, will he? I disabled the shortwave radio, so you won't be able to call anyone. As soon as your dad wires the money to me in the Caymans, I'll tell him where to find you. I promise I will."

"You'll never get away with this, you know."

Pete laughed mockingly and said, "I'm smarter than that. I have it all planned out. The money will go to a numbered account in the Caymans. The Cayman banks make the Swiss bankers look talkative. But I have it set for an automatic transfer to the Bahamas, and they don't have an extradition treaty with the US. I won't ever come back to the States, but I know a guy who can alter the registration on this plane, and I can make a very good living in the Islands. I'll do okay. By the way, don't bother trying to switch to transmit rather than intercom. I turned off the radio, so you won't be able to reach anyone." Pete laughed again and in falsetto mocked, "Please fasten your seatbelts and return your seats to the upright and locked position. Thank you for flying Romson Air."

Jed felt the plane flare, and the floats splashed in the lake and bounced before splashing once again as Pete chopped the throttle and turned the plane toward the dock. Elizabeth raised her head finally and looked fearfully out the window to see the lodge just beyond the dock. Pete carefully eased the plane alongside the dock, quickly jumped from the plane, and secured it in place.

Pete opened the passenger door and then handed Elizabeth the handcuff key. He pulled his pistol from his pocket and told her to unlock her handcuff. It had been an uncomfortable trip sitting hunched over as they were. Pete forced Jed to unload the luggage and then handcuffed his hands behind him. "You know where the rifles are in the lodge, and I'm not about to let you try to stop me." Pete looked down at the dock and shuffled his feet before continuing. "I told you I don't want you hurt, and that is the truth. Your family has always been good to me, and I feel terrible about what I'm doing. But it is my life if I don't. I ask you to understand."

He turned to Elizabeth. "Missy, you walk off of the dock and sit down. I'll leave this key inside your purse here on the dock. After I take off, you may come back down here, get the key, and release Jed. I'm sorry you got involved in this, but I had no choice. It's just your bad luck, I guess. You will be okay. Your parents will know where you two are just as soon as Jed's dad wires the money to me. I told Jed about the supplies in the cabin, so you won't go hungry or be cold. Goodbye."

Pete waited for Elizabeth to walk the length of the dock and sit before he quickly loosed the moorings on the plane, jumped in, started the engine, and slowly eased out onto the lake. He gave them a wave as he left, but neither Jed nor Elizabeth responded from where they were seated at the end of the dock.

CHAPTER 4

O fficer Sorrells flipped on his lights behind the illegally parked car. There was still no sign of life or activity. Too bad the owner would have to pay the towing fees, but he had to do his job. He had already waited a lot longer than he should have. Officer Sorrells called it in and started the paperwork while he waited for Crook Autobody to bring their flatbed truck and tow the car. He always tried to use as much leniency as he could on these deals. Having a broken-down car was bad enough, but getting a ticket for illegal parking when it couldn't be helped just added insult to injury.

He had no way of knowing Pete's car would never be claimed.

CHAPTER 5

A n old Canada goose sat on her nest, having just laid her first egg of the season. The noise of the airplane's engine close by on the lake disturbed her to the point that she did not notice a coyote creeping up on her. When the coyote rushed, she frantically launched into flight over the water as Pete pulled back on the yoke and lifted the plane into the air. Pete saw the goose fly in front of him at the wrong moment. He had insufficient airspeed to maneuver, but, instinctively, he wrenched the yoke to the left, trying desperately to avoid the goose, but there wasn't enough time, airspeed, or altitude. She struck the propeller and shattered one of the blades, throwing the racing engine out of balance, and, at the same time, the left wingtip touched the surface of the water, cartwheeling the plane across the surface. Pete's head struck the doorpost, and he lost consciousness as the plane came apart around him. Only a few feathers and one broken float remained on the roiled water. A burst of bubbles and a little oil broke the surface, but nothing else was left to mark the spot where the plane went down.

Horrified, Elizabeth and Jed stared on in disbelief.

CHAPTER 6

harles Sitton drove his ten-year-old Oldsmobile into his driveway and parked with a sigh. He was so glad to be home and see Elizabeth! It seemed she had been gone much longer than ten days. Charles was surprised to see no lights on in the house but surmised that Elizabeth had been tired and was taking a nap while awaiting his return from work. He hurried to the front door and unlocked it, calling, "Lizzie, I'm home!" No response. He walked down the hallway to her room, expecting to find her lying down, but she was not there, nor was there any sign she had been home. Concerned, he grabbed the phone.

James Romson had remained at the plant to help oversee the repairs on the assembly line along with Charles Sitton, so he was just walking in the door of his own home when the phone rang. He picked it up and answered, "Romson residence."

"James, Charles here. Did Jed get the message to give Elizabeth a ride home today? She isn't here yet."

"I don't know, Charles. I just walked in the door. I didn't see his Bronco in the drive. Hang on and I'll ask Mary if she's heard from him."

In the background, Charles heard, "Mary? I'm home. Have you heard from Jed?"

Mary Romson walked into the kitchen where James held the telephone. "Hi, James." She gave him a quick peck on the cheek. "I've not heard from Jed. Did their plane get in on time?"

James Romson spoke into the telephone again. "Charles, Mary hasn't heard from them. Do you know if they arrived back at the school yet?"

"The bus was at the school when I drove by, so they had to have gotten in. I didn't see many cars in the parking lot. You know they wouldn't hang around there long. I'll call their sponsor, Mr. Johnson, at home and see if he knows anything." With his finger, Charles broke the connection. He picked up the directory and quickly looked up George Johnson's phone number.

"Johnsons'" was the tired-sounding response he heard after the second ring.

"Mr. Johnson, Charles Sitton here. Do you know if Elizabeth got the word to ride home with Jed Romson this morning? She isn't here at the house."

"Hi, Charles. Please, call me George. The kids call me 'Mr.' I know Elizabeth got the word. I saw her get in the car with Jed. They didn't waste any time leaving, but I don't know where they went. As far as I know, everyone went home. I didn't hear anything about anyone going anywhere else."

"Did anyone else ride with them?"

"I don't know. I didn't see anyone else get in the car, but I can't say for sure. I know Elizabeth was unhappy you weren't there."

"I know. It couldn't be helped. We had a hydraulic line burst at the plant, and it started a small fire. James and I both had to go in and get it taken care of. Thanks for your time, and welcome home."

"You might try the Baldwins. Teddy was sitting with Jed on the bus. He would know if they had any other plans." George sounded hopeful.

"Thanks, again." Charles Sitton again broke the connection and looked up the Baldwins' phone number. After six rings, the answering machine picked up. Charles hung up the phone and tried to think who else might know where Jed and Elizabeth could be. Perhaps Samantha would know. She and Elizabeth were very close. He wiped his forehead with the back of his hand and wrist. For some reason, he was sweating and dread pooled in his stomach.

Finding the Quarlles' number, finally, he dialed. On the third ring, he heard "Hello?"

"Hi, Mr. Quarlles? Charles Sitton here. Could I speak with Samantha?"

"I'm sorry, but you have the wrong number."

"Sorry!" Frustrated, he hung up and carefully redialed the Quarlles' number.

"Hello, Quarlles' residence."

"Hi. This is Charles Sitton. Could I please speak with Samantha for just a moment?"

"Certainly, just a jiffy."

Charles poured himself a glass of cold water and sat down at the kitchen table. His hands shook. He knew he was being ridiculous and jumping to conclusions, but anxiety had overtaken him. Elizabeth would probably call him a worrywart when she walked in.

"Hi, Mr. Sitton. This is Samantha."

"Oh, hi, Samantha. Welcome home. I hope you enjoyed your trip."

"Oh, yes! Thanks! We had a great time."

"Good. Quick question for you. Do you know if Elizabeth rode home with Jed?"

"Yes, I know she did. I saw her get in his truck. She seemed upset about something."

"I know. I was supposed to pick her up, but we had a breakdown. Do you know if anyone else went with them or if they said anything about stopping somewhere first?"

"I'm sorry, but I didn't talk to her after we got off the bus. I don't think anyone else rode along, though. I didn't see anyone else."

"Thanks very much. Welcome home, and I'll see you at graduation."

"Okay, I can't wait! You are coming to my party, aren't you?"

"Wouldn't miss it! See you then." With a shaking hand, he hung up one more time, then dialed the number every parent dreads.

"Police Department, Sergeant Donnelly speaking. How may I help you?"

"Hello, Sergeant. Charles Sitton here. I'm calling to see if there have been any accident reports or any incidents involving my daughter, Elizabeth, and Jed Romson. Jed would have been driving an old Ford Bronco, blue with a white top. I'm sorry, but I don't know the year or license number. They should have been home, and . . ."

"No, sir. I've had no accident reports today at all. It's been a quiet day."

"Thanks. My daughter should have returned home hours ago, but neither she nor Jed have been seen or heard from. What should I do?"

"How old is she?"

"She just turned eighteen last month."

"Do you suspect foul play? You mentioned a Jed Romson. Do you suspect he did something?"

"No, they are classmates and friends. I don't suspect Jed of hurting her."

"Well, sir, she is an adult, so unless there is reason to believe a crime or foul play has been committed, there is really nothing we can do. Sometimes kids do crazy things. I'm sure she'll turn up."

"Okay, thank you, sir. I appreciate your help." Charles Sitton hung up the phone and sank into a chair with a worried frown. This was so unlike Elizabeth. He couldn't imagine her wanting to go someplace or do anything before coming home.

He picked up the phone again and dialed the Romson home. "Hello, Mary? Charles here. Have you heard anything from Jed?"

"Charles, I'm sorry, but we haven't heard from him. We've been trying to find him, too."

"I just got off the phone with the police. They don't have any accident reports or anything. They said they can't do anything unless a crime or foul play has been committed because they both are considered adults. I guess we just have to wait for them to show up."

It was a long, sleepless night in both homes.

CHAPTER 7

Jed and Elizabeth were somber, and Elizabeth sniffled as they walked up the hill to the lodge. What would they do now? With the plane gone and Pete gone, no one would come to the lodge any time soon. Pete said he would reveal where they were when he got the money, but that was never going to happen now. Pete said he disabled the shortwave radio, but Jed could check. Maybe he could make it work somehow.

Jed pushed the lodge door open and stepped back for Elizabeth to enter. The room was rather chilly, so a fire was the first order of business. It was a standing rule that no one ever left the lodge without a fire laid in the fireplace ready to be lit. One never knew when the next person would arrive, and, in inclement weather, having a fire ready could be the difference between life or death. Jed took the box of matches from the mantel and quickly kindled a fire.

"Take a look around, Lizzie. I'll go get our gear."

There was not a lot to see. It was a huge old log cabin, once used for a logging camp, but abandoned when it was determined there was a lot of timber to be accessed much more easily and cheaply. The area was simply not conducive to road-building through marshes and small streams. The Romsons improved the cabin quite a bit, but it was still rustic. From the doorway, Lizzie could see, in the middle of the right wall, a large fireplace built of native stone with a wide, thick, rough-hewn oak mantel. Over the mantel was a stuffed moose head with antlers at least six feet wide. Lizzie hated stuffed animal heads like this. They always seemed to be watching her, creeping her out. A shudder ran through her shoulders.

A fireplace crane on the left side fireplace wall could suspend a pot over the fire, and the andirons were made with a spit for roasting meat. On the other side of the fireplace, a counter with an overhanging top and three rough stools on either side made an ell into the room.

An old porcelain sink with no faucet was on the end wall. In the back corner, just beyond the sink, a large pantry with open shelves had an assortment of bags, boxes, and cans. It looked like they shouldn't go hungry, for a few days anyway.

On the back wall, next to the pantry, was a huge cast iron wood stove. Lizzie was accustomed to cooking for her dad at home, but that was with a gas range. How on earth could she be expected to make that thing work? A big tear trickled down her face and made a splotch on her shirt when it dripped from her chin. She slumped onto one of the stools and buried her face in her hands on the counter and sobbed.

The eight sets of bunks and a big pot-bellied stove on the other end of the lodge were unnoticed in her grief.

There was nothing fancy about the lodge. It was designed for rough living, without any frills. It was clean and neat, but it was far more spartan than anything she had ever seen, even when "roughing it" in Girl Scouts.

Jed walked into the lodge with a backpack slung over each shoulder, and he dragged their roller cases behind him. "Not bad for a home away from home, huh? It's nothing fancy, I know, but it will keep the rain off of us until we can get home."

Lizzie turned to look at him through bleary eyes and, as much as she struggled not to, wailed "Oh, Jed! What are we going to do?"

"Right now, I suggest we call it a night and get some sleep. I know we are both exhausted after the flight—well, both of them. It has been a long, long day. I don't think we should make any decisions tonight. We will both think much more clearly in the morning. That area over there, with the curtain, is for you. We don't normally have women come up here, but on occasion Mom or one of the other wives will come along. The little room in the back is actually a bathroom, although it is nothing like you've ever seen." Jed smiled. "Let me show you how it works."

He led Lizzie to the back of the room and opened the door. "As soon as I go outside and turn it on, there is a stream of water running continuously into the lavatory. It comes from a spring up the hill and flows all the time, both here and in the kitchen sink. In the winter, it has to be turned off if the lodge is not in use. But otherwise, the pipe is buried far enough to keep it flowing, and it flows enough it doesn't freeze. The toilet has to be filled with a bucket."

"You've got to be kidding me! What did you get me into?" Lizzie stomped her foot in frustration.

"Sorry, but that is the best we could do without power available to us. That little tub is a bathtub. It came out of a mini-camper, and since we don't have a hot water heater, you don't take long baths!" He laughed, self-conscious. "We carry hot water back here, and there is a diverter at the sink to run water to the tub. Since it is hard to carry hot water, we don't use it much. Most of the time, when we are up here, we are hunting, so we don't care. Not bathing much helps with the scent issue for the game."

The scowl on Lizzie's face showed what she thought.

Exasperated, Jed pointed. "You can grab a sleeping bag from the shelf, and there are clean sheets available in the cupboard. You should stay warm enough. If you would be good enough to say something to be sure I'm decent before coming out of your curtain, it would be appreciated. Good night. Call me if you need anything." Jed tried not to let it show in his voice, but his irritation bled through.

"And what do we do about lights?" The question was bitter.

"Oh, thanks, I forgot. You will find a wind-up flashlight on the shelf right by the bunks. You can use it if you need to get up during the night. We also have Coleman lanterns that we use for light in the lodge. Anything else?"

"I don't think so. I'm going to bed before anything else happens to me."

"Call me if you need anything." Jed shook his head. This was going to be interesting. Not only did he have to babysit a tenderfoot, he had to listen to her, too.

Lizzie didn't think she would be able to sleep a wink, but when she put her head on the pillow, the next thing she knew sunlight was shining in her eyes, and the smell of coffee was in the air.

CHAPTER 8

J ames Romson stirred and lifted his head from his hands where his face was cradled. His elbows ached from resting on the tabletop and supporting his head. The sunrise was shining in the kitchen window, brightening the room with a cheery orange glow. Its beauty, however, was lost upon him and Mary as they sat where they had been all night long.

"Why don't you start some coffee and breakfast? It's seven o'clock. I think I'll call Charles and ask him to come over. Maybe we can think of what needs to be done while we eat."

"Would omelets be okay?"

"Sounds good to me."

James picked up the phone and dialed. "Morning, Charles. Mary's making omelets. Why don't you come over for breakfast, and let's see if we can make some sense of what's going on. . . . No, don't worry about cleaning up first. We've both been up all night, so we're in the same shape. . . . Fine, see you in about fifteen, then."

Charles drove his Oldsmobile carefully into the Romsons' driveway. Normally, he would not be seen outside his door like this. Totally disheveled with shirt half untucked, one shoe untied, unshaven, hair catawampus on his head, eyes bleary from lack of sleep, and shoulders slumped with defeat, Charles half-stumbled as he rounded the front of his car. He was beyond caring how he looked. Charles was not a drinking man, which was good because he surely would have "crawled into a bottle" at this point. Having lost his wife of twenty-one years just three years before, to now lose his eighteen-year-old daughter was too much. Head down, he shuffled to the front door.

James, having heard the car, opened the door for him.

"Good morning, Charles. Thanks for coming over."

"Thanks for calling. I don't mind saying I'm at my wit's end. I haven't slept a wink." Wearily, he rubbed his eyes with the knuckles of one hand. "I appreciate the offer of breakfast. I ate nothing last night; eating wasn't even on my mind."

"I thought that might be the case, and I thought if we could put our heads together, we might come up with ideas on which way to go." James took his arm and led him into the kitchen; Charles pulled out a chair and wearily sat down.

Mary slid a cup of coffee in front of him. "Omelets will be ready in just a couple of minutes." She still had a bit of a sense of propriety. She had taken a few minutes to wash her face, erase the tear lines from her mascara, and brush her hair. She hadn't taken the time for makeup.

James took a pad of paper and a pen from the counter behind him and sat down heavily at the head of the table. "I thought we might write down ideas and what we've done so we don't waste time and energy duplicating each other. Sound like a good idea to you, Charles?"

"Sure. Don't have much idea where to start, though. The PD doesn't seem to think it is too serious. The sergeant I talked with seemed to think they just ran off together. He said kids do crazy stuff like that, but I don't see Elizabeth doing it, and Jed doesn't strike me as one who would be so irresponsible either."

James nodded. "I know. I think we ought to check Jed's credit card, just in case. Does Elizabeth carry a card?"

"I sent one with her, in case of emergency," Charles said and smiled his thanks as Mary slid a hot omelet in front of him. "My doctor would have a conniption if she saw me eating this omelet, but I don't care! It smells good."

Mary put her hand on his shoulder and gave it a gentle squeeze. "Thanks. It's three-cheese, and I have bacon coming in just a minute."

"That would really set her off!"

James nodded his thanks also and wrote down *Credit cards* on his pad. "What else do we need to do?"

Mary came back to the table with a plate of bacon and the coffeepot. As she refilled cups, she said, "I think we need to talk to the rest of the kids and the adults on the trip. Someone may know something. I know you talked with a few last night, but one of the others might know something the others didn't."

Call kids, James wrote.

"I didn't reach anyone at the Baldwins'," Charles said. "Someone said Jed and the Baldwin kid were sitting together on the bus."

"Yeah, they are pretty close," said James. "Let's bless the food." He bowed his head. "Our Father, we give thanks for this, our food, and we beg your guidance in finding our children."

CHAPTER 9

Elizabeth sat up in her bunk and stretched. The coffee smelled good. She was amazed at how well she had slept, but their circumstances rushed back into her consciousness as wakefulness entered. They had decisions to make.

Jed awoke early and lay in his bunk thinking about what needed to be done. He felt responsible for Lizzie. It was because of him she was stranded. He also knew she was not accustomed to the sort of lifestyle they would have to live until rescue came. Rescue might be within a day or two, or it could be months. He must plan on months. Obviously, they would have to work together. Based on last night's experience, he didn't have a lot of hope for that to happen.

Because they were in the same small class in school, they spent a lot of time together; however, he didn't know Lizzie all that well. Outside of class and an occasional ride home, they didn't have much in common and didn't hang out together. He was going to have to get to know Lizzie a lot better before this was all over.

He rose and started coffee, trying to be as quiet as possible so as to not awaken her. He knew she would need all the strength she could muster to get through this. He sat down at the table with a notepad and his cup of coffee and started jotting down what needed to be done: *Inventory supplies, examine the 2-way radio to see if it can be fixed, devise a way of signaling anyone flying overhead . . .* He paused as Lizzie called out and then opened her curtain.

"Coffee smells good."

"How do you drink yours?"

"A little sugar, thanks." Jed set a cup in front of Lizzie as she sat down at the table. "Look, I'm sorry for the way I acted last night. It's not your fault I'm here. I'm scared, and I don't know what I'm doing. Besides that, I miss Daddy."

Jed looked at Lizzie thoughtfully for a moment. "It's okay, Lizzie. I appreciate the apology, but I wasn't at my best last night either. We'll put that behind us and go from here. First order of business is breakfast. We have some pastries that Pete brought up. Will they do? I haven't had time to see what options we have yet, and pastries won't last long."

"They will be fine," Lizzie sighed.

"Then we have to figure out how we are going to get by until we are rescued."

"Can't we hike out of here? Maybe find someone fishing on the lake or something?" She sounded panicked.

"No. The lake is all on our property, so there won't be anyone on it. We can't hike out either. This part of Maine has less than one person per hundred square miles. Dad bought this land to be sure it was as remote as we could get it. Quebec is to our west and north, and New Brunswick is to our east. I'm not sure how far, but it is a ways. The nearest small town is over fifty miles away, and there are lakes, rivers, and a lot of marshes, plus some small mountains we would have to cross or go around. I know of two hunting camps, but the closest one is about thirty-five miles from here, and I'm not sure exactly where it is. No, whatever happens, we have to prepare for it."

"Do you think anyone will ever find us?" Lizzie started to cry.

"Oh, don't worry about that! Someone will be up here; we just don't know how soon. Remember, Dad doesn't have a plane or a pilot anymore, and they won't think of looking up here, I'm sure. I'm sure our dads have the police searching for us, but they will be looking down there. Dad can't still have the managers' fishing trip next week, and, except for the goose hunt in September, there is nothing else on the schedule for the year—other than if someone wanted to come up here on vacation—but then again, no plane. Someone will be up here sooner or later; we just have to plan on it being a while."

"What will we do for food? I know Pete brought supplies, but not how much."

"I know. I started looking a little bit at what we have. You know more about cooking than I do. Maybe you could check out what we have? I'm not worried about having enough to eat. I've been hunting up here since I was little, and I've set snares, too, for small game and furs. Plus, there are plenty of fish in the lake, and it hardly gets fished, so it isn't hard to catch fish."

"Okay, but what about wolves and other wild animals?"

"There aren't any wolves in Maine anymore. Conservationists and animal rights people have been talking about trying to reintroduce them, but they haven't yet. There are coyotes, but coyotes usually won't bother you. There are some cougars and bobcats, but they are more scared of you than you are of them. They hardly ever bother humans. You might hear one at night, but it isn't anything to worry about.

"Black bears are a different matter. They normally don't bother you unless they have a cub or you corner them. The best thing to do if you see one is just to walk away quietly, and don't run. They can run faster than you can, and they also climb trees, so you can't get away from them that way. I've seen bears up here, but I've never had a problem with one.

"I always carry a rifle with me when I'm out in the woods, just in case, but in all the years I've come up here I've never needed it other than for game. Just stay with me if you go into the woods until you are comfortable on your own." Jed paused and then said, "For now, let's focus on seeing what we have and figure out how to make it stretch."

"I know one thing that will be a problem!"

"Oh? What?"

"Clothes! I don't have much I can wear here! Most of the time in Europe was fairly dressy. I only have one pair of jeans, and my other stuff won't hold up long."

"There are a few things in the cold weather gear we can maybe make work for you temporarily. If I can get a couple of deer, I can make buckskin and some clothes from it. It won't be fancy, and I'm not doing any Indian quill work or anything like that, but they will be clothes."

CHAPTER 10

harles Sitton picked up the phone and called the Baldwin home. "Hello, Sam. Charles Sitton here. Say, I'm sorry to be calling so early on Saturday morning, but I tried to get Teddy last night, and I didn't get an answer. Is he available this morning? . . . Thanks, I'll be happy to wait."

Charles sat and stared at the phone for an excruciating five minutes while the Romsons watched.

"Hi, Teddy. So sorry to wake you, but I need a little help. Did Jed say anything to you about going anywhere when you got back?"

"No, sir. He was in a hurry to get home. I think we all were. I know he had to take Lizzie home, but that is on his way anyhow."

"Okay, thanks." Charles struggled with what he had to say next, and his voice broke. "Neither he nor Elizabeth arrived at home."

"Oh, no! I'm sorry! What can I do to help?"

"Right now, nothing. We are just contacting you guys that were on the trip with them to see if you know of anything that might help us find them. If you think of anything at all, even if it isn't something you think important, please give me a call, or call the Romsons if I'm not at home."

"Will do, sir. I'm really sorry! I'll talk with you later."

Charles hung up the phone, shook his head, and picked up the directory.

"Charles, why don't we split the numbers," asked James, "and I'll make some calls on the office line here? Maybe we can save some time and frustration."

"Okay, good idea."

Charles turned to Mary. "Mary, could I trouble you for another cup of coffee?" Mary filled his cup and then topped off her own and her husband's while they divided the list of names. James picked up his cup and list and walked into the office as Charles grabbed the kitchen phone and called the Alexanders. "Hi, Sandy, Charles Sitton here. I hate to call you at home so early on Saturday, but I need some help. Neither Jed nor Elizabeth got home last night. Did you hear either of them, or one of the other kids, say anything about going somewhere else?"

"Oh, no! That's terrible! No, I didn't hear anything. Everyone seemed to be anxious to get home right away. Did you call the police?"

"Yes, I called them last night, but since they both are eighteen, the police can't do anything unless there is foul play. As far as the law goes, there isn't anything they can do."

"I'm so sorry! Please let us know what you find out, will you?"

"Sure thing. Thanks." Again, he hung up the phone with fear swelling in his chest.

CHAPTER 11

Jed and Lizzie spent the morning inventorying their supplies and looking through the cold weather gear left at the cabin. There was a fair supply of canned goods and pancake mixes, flour, sugar, pasta, and assorted other supplies. They figured there was enough there to last them for two to three months if they were careful. What was lacking was meat, although there were a few pounds of bacon and three dozen eggs. Those would have to be used soon since they were perishable. Jed reminded Lizzie not to worry about meat; he would set snares. There were plenty of fish to be caught, and, although it wasn't hunting season, he didn't think it would be wrong to do a little hunting.

Though Jed was careful not to say anything negative to Lizzie, he was certain no one would be up there looking for them anytime soon. Because Romson Industries did not allow anyone other than employees or close business associates to hunt or fish on the property, there would be no one coming to use the lodge. Since Pete and the plane were gone, the company would not have a plane for traveling to the lodge either. Jed was sure the insurance would replace the plane eventually, but since no one knew Pete had crashed, there would be a time lapse before anything could be done. At a minimum of half a million dollars to replace the plane, he knew his dad would not be going out to buy one anytime soon. The loss of Jed and Lizzie would also dampen the desire of either of their fathers to visit the property for hunting or fishing: he had to plan for a long stay.

CHAPTER 12

James Romson walked from his home office with slumped shoulders. "Did you get anything, Charles?"

"Not a thing. Neither Jed nor Lizzie said anything to anyone. They just got in the Bronco and disappeared."

The three worried parents sat around the table and talked about what could be done. It appeared the police could be of no help. They couldn't even put out a "BOLO," or "Be on the Lookout," for the Bronco since the truck was in Jed's name. The parents seemed to be at an impasse. Articles in newspapers? Posters on light poles? Nothing seemed to fit what was needed.

The phone rang. Mary answered and handed the receiver to Charles. "It's for you. I think it's Teddy Baldwin."

"Hi, Mr. Sitton. It's Teddy. I don't know if this is important or not, but I just remembered there was a car broken down on the 'No Parking' side of the street by the school. I saw Jed stop and talk with the guy, and then the guy got in the Bronco with them. I didn't see who he was, but Jed seemed to know him."

"Thanks, Teddy! That is exactly what I was talking about! Let me know if you think of anything else."

"I think we have something!" Charles exclaimed. "Teddy saw Jed pick someone up by the school drive. Let's run over and see if we can find out whose car it is." The three parents jumped up from the table and started for the door. "Let's take mine," said Charles. "It's in the drive." They piled in the car, and Charles backed quickly out of the driveway. It was a tense fifteen minutes with each of the parents lost in their own thoughts. At last, the school came into sight, but when they got to the traffic light and looked left down the street, they saw no car. Their hopes were immediately dashed. Charles felt tears welling up in his eyes again at the disappointment. He had been so hopeful for an answer, but . . .

"Drive us to the police station," James ordered. "Let me talk with the chief. We go back a long ways together. He may have some ideas."

Charles made a U-turn when the light changed and drove back toward downtown. As they pulled up in front of the police department, Mary asked if he had any tissues; Charles pulled a small packet from the glove box and handed them to her. She wiped her eyes and blew her nose before getting out of the car. Together, they walked into the lobby and to the desk officer.

"How may I help you?" asked the officer.

"We would like to speak with Chief Washington for a moment," said James.

"May I ask what you need? I may be able to help you."

"Actually, we need advice concerning a situation, but, no offense, I don't believe you can help. Chief Washington is an old friend of mine, and I trust his counsel. I know it is an imposition, but the situation needs to be addressed right away."

"Okay, sir. May I have your name, and I'll see if he is available. He may be in the staff meeting."

"Tell him James Romson is here to see him. I think he will break the meeting for me, and I promise not to waste his time."

The officer picked up the phone and dialed a number from memory. "Hello, Diane, is the boss in? I have a Mr. Romson here who needs to see him. He says it's important."

There was a pause before the desk officer said, "Okay, thanks. I'll tell them." He looked up at James. "His secretary asked you to hold for about five minutes for the boss to put an end to the meeting, and he said he will be right down. Why don't you have a seat?"

James led Mary and Charles over to what looked like old church pews, and they sat. The chief came bustling through the door behind the desk not two minutes after they sat. The officer stood, surprised, and then looked with interest at the Romsons. He had expected the chief to have them go to his office. These must be very special people.

"James! Mary! What can I do for you today?" He walked around the counter and hugged Mary before shaking James's hand.

"Jeff, sorry to interrupt your meeting, but we need your help."

"Not a problem! I hate getting bogged down in them anyway, and I liked having an excuse to leave."

"I'd like you to meet Charles Sitton, another old friend of mine, and head of maintenance for Romson Industries."

The chief shook Charles's hand. "Pleased to meet you, Charles, but I really don't think this is a social call. What can I do for you?"

"Could we take it to your office or someplace else private?"

"Certainly. Come with me."

James turned to the desk officer. "Thank you very much for your help, sir. We appreciate it." He then turned to the chief. "My compliments on this officer. He was very courteous and helpful."

The chief nodded at the officer and grinned. "Good. I like to hear that. Jack's been on light duty since getting hurt in a fight with a guy he arrested. Maybe we can keep him here since he's doing such a good job."

He laughed at the look of horror on the young officer's face and waved for them to follow him behind the counter, through the door, and to his office. "Diane, if the mayor calls while we are busy, please tell him I will call him back. We are not to be disturbed unless the president calls."

Diane laughed and nodded her head.

He closed the door behind them. "What's going on?"

James said, "We need some advice, Jeff. I know there is nothing you can do officially, but Jed and Elizabeth—Charles's daughter—didn't get home last night from their senior trip. Charles called here last evening and was told there was nothing you could do since they are both over eighteen, and there was no sign of foul play." The chief nodded in agreement.

"The sergeant Charles spoke with said it isn't uncommon for kids to just take off and then show up later."

The chief nodded again. "Um-hmm. We can file a missing person's report after they've been gone twenty-four hours, but if we find them, all we can do is tell them you're concerned and ask them to contact you. Then we can let you know we have spoken with them, and they are safe."

James nodded. "Well, this morning we contacted all of the people on the trip to see if either Jed or Elizabeth said anything to anyone about going somewhere else, but they hadn't. A while later, one of the young men called back and said he saw Jed stop at the end of the school drive and talk with a man with a broken-down car. He then got into the truck with them. We just went by the school, but there was no car. Would there, by any chance, be any record of a car parked on the wrong side of the street? We thought maybe we could find out who they talked with."

The chief reached for the phone. "Diane, would you pull all incident reports for yesterday from . . . hold one." He looked at James. "What time did they return?"

"I'm not sure. Probably about eight or eight-thirty. They were supposed to return before school started."

The chief nodded and then spoke into the phone again. "Try from seven-thirty until noon. See if there was anything about a car parked on the wrong side of Higgins between Sixty-third and Sixty-fifth. Let me know what you find. Thanks." He set the phone back in the cradle.

"Let's give her a few minutes to check the incident reports. Can I offer you a cup of coffee while we wait?"

"Thanks, Jeff; coffee would be great," said James. "We've been up all night."

The chief swiveled his chair and poured four cups of coffee from the pot on his credenza. "I learned when I took this job to have my own coffee in here. Nobody around here knows how to make good coffee, it seems."

James laughed. "Jeff doesn't think any civilian knows how to make good coffee. If it isn't Navy style, it isn't any good. I can't argue, though. I learned to like Navy coffee when I was on the boats as a Marine. Seems like a different lifetime, though."

"You gotta put a little pinch of salt in it," said the chief. He answered the phone before it finished its first ring. "What do you have? Um-hmm. Okay, thanks."

As Chief Washington hung up the phone, he said, "Diane said a car was picked up by the school just before eleven yesterday morning, registered to a Pete Richardson."

James visibly paled at the name. "Pete is our company pilot. Jed would have picked him up without question."

"Is that a problem?"

"I hope not, but I'm not sure. Pete was in to see me yesterday, wanting to borrow quite a large chunk of money. I refused to loan the money to him. I hope he didn't do something stupid."

The chief nodded solemnly. "At this time, there is really nothing I can do officially, but I will pass the word to the force to keep an eye out. We can file the missing person reports later this afternoon if you don't find them." He took a business card from the holder on his desk and wrote a number on it. "This is my direct line. You know my home number. I want you to let me know whatever you find out just as soon as you know anything. Any time, day or night, do you hear me? I don't care if it's the middle of the night. You know how highly we think of Jed."

"Got it, Jeff. Thank you so much for your time."

CHAPTER 13

J ed showed Lizzie how to light the cookstove. She was nervous, having never used anything other than the gas range at home. The biggest problem with the stove was it could not be turned off like a gas stove, so it stayed on and put out a lot of heat all the time. In the winter, heat was a good thing, but in the summer it could get quite hot in the kitchen. This model included a hot water tank, so heating water wasn't as much of a chore. They just had to be careful not to let it run dry.

"Come outside with me, and I'll show you another fireplace for cooking. We use it in the summer to keep the cabin cool." Jed led her outside to a brick fireplace, built much like the wood stove, but without the hot water tank. "It has a brick oven attached so we can bake or roast without roasting ourselves." The best Jed could get from her was a wan smile.

"Over here is a fire pit we use when we want to sit around a fire at night. We also use the spit to roast large pieces of meat. I think I'll build a rack instead though to smoke and dry meat and fish when we get more than we will eat. We can make jerky, too. I know dried meat isn't the most exciting thing, but there will be times we need it, and we can't refrigerate anything."

"How do you make jerky? I've had beef jerky a few times, and I liked it." Lizzie showed her first spark of interest, fleeting though it was.

"Wait until I get a deer and I'll show you. It's not that hard. It just takes time." Jed could tell Lizzie was trying hard to keep up a good attitude, but it was clear she was out of her depth.

He led the way around the cabin to a built-on lean-to storage area where two canoes were stored along with fishing gear and tackle. In the back sat several boxes of clothing.

"Most of these will be too big for you, and some of them will be too hot to wear during the day in the summer, but they might be good for evenings and mornings. We'll just take them inside, and you can go through them and see what you can use. I'll probably need a few things, too, although I have some stuff I leave up here. Come to think of it, I'll bet I've outgrown them. Some of those might fit you."

They carried the boxes into the cabin and dropped them on an empty bunk. Jed said, "We can check these out later. Let me show you around the area while it is nice out."

Lizzie dropped into a deerskin-bound chair and buried her face in her hands. "I don't think I can do this, Jed. I'm not cut out to be a Swiss Family Robinson character. I'm not an outdoorsy type of girl. This is all well and good for you, but you grew up with this stuff. I don't have any idea what I'm doing." Her voice was muffled by her hands, but her words weren't what disturbed Jed the most. He was concerned about her defeated attitude.

"Come on, Lizzie. It's not that bad. We can do this if we do it together. I'll teach you everything you need to know. What other choice do we have?"

Obviously, that was the wrong question, for it set off a fresh round of tears and sobs. Jed sighed with frustration.

CHAPTER 14

Charles Sitton parked his car by the hangar and the three of them hurried from the car. They saw no sign of life around the hangar— no cars or people. James pulled his keys from his pocket and walked to the door, but he was puzzled to find his key would not fit into the lock. He checked to be certain he had the correct key and tried again. Again, the key would not insert. "Charles, did we have this lock changed? My key won't fit."

Charles walked over. "Not that I know of. I didn't get a purchase order from Pete. Here, try mine." His key did not fit either. "I don't like the looks of this. We'd better go back to the plant and get my tools."

Mary spoke up. "I think we should call the police. I don't like the looks of this either. If Pete is up to something—though I can't imagine what—we had better protect any evidence."

"Good thinking, honey. Let's get Charles's tools and a phone. I'll call and get an officer out here."

They retraced their steps and drove the short distance to Romson Industries' plant offices. James and Mary hurried to make the call while

Charles went to the maintenance office and threw some tools into a bag to dismantle the lock. He also threw in a replacement door latch. Charles returned to the car shortly after James and Mary. James, visibly agitated, leaned across the seat. "We will probably have to wait a while. The sergeant at the desk didn't seem very impressed with the need to have someone here. I don't think he would have agreed to send someone if I had not said I would call the chief if he didn't. He said, 'Everyone is busy'; but there is busy, and then there is I-don't-want-to-be-bothered-busy. I really don't understand it. Normally, when we ask for help, they are very responsive."

After twenty long minutes, a patrol car cruised sedately into the drive at the hangar and eased to a stop next to Charles's car. A young officer stepped out and introduced himself.

"Hello, I'm Officer John Donovan. I don't know what I can do for you. Didn't the sergeant explain we don't do lockout service?"

"We didn't ask for lockout service," James exploded. "I didn't think he was listening to me! We asked for an officer because our kids are missing and were last seen with my pilot. Now, the door to the hangar has been tampered with. We wanted someone to be available because something is wrong."

"I'm sorry! Sarge is usually better than that. It seems his mind just isn't there all the time. It's a personal issue he's going through. When did you report them missing?" Officer Donovan pulled a notebook from his shirt pocket and started taking notes. "Please understand some questions you will be asked may seem offensive, but we have to ask. First, let's take a look at the door."

The four of them walked over to the entry door, and James pulled out his keys. He handed them to Officer Donovan, who tried to insert the key into the lock. When it would not go, even though he jiggled it around and tried to force it, he knelt on the ground and looked at the keyhole. "Um-hmm," he said. He pulled a small penlight from his duty belt and shined it at the lock. "I thought so. Someone squirted Super Glue, or something like it, into the lock. You won't be able to open this lock again. Do you have a locksmith you can call to cut the lock off?"

"No need," said Charles. "I've got the tools right here." He pulled a cordless drill from the bag and drilled the lock mechanism from the handle, and then using a small screwdriver, he reached inside the knob and retracted the latch. Carefully holding the latch open he pulled on the door. James stepped in first followed by Officer Donovan and Mary. James flipped on the light switch and they saw Jed's Bronco, but the plane was missing.

Mary Romson wailed, "Oh no!" and sank to her knees on the floor. James Romson knelt down beside her and put his arm around her shoulders, pulling her to his chest. He buried his head in her hair and whispered, "Hang on, babe. We'll get through this. We'll get Jed back."

Charles Sitton stood frozen, stunned at the development. He felt all alone. With his wife so recently gone, now to have lost Elizabeth was overwhelming. He felt as if he had been punched violently in the chest and found his breath hard to catch. His face went ashen, and his hands shook with emotion.

Charles fell to the floor. Officer Donovan immediately checked Charles's pulse while talking in his radio, calling for an ambulance and backup. Charles kept mumbling, "If I would have been there, she would be okay. If I would have been there, she would be okay," while Officer Donovan kept telling him, "Take it easy. You're gonna be all right" and "Stay with me." It was only minutes, but it seemed like hours before an ambulance came screaming up the drive. Paramedics hurried through the door, followed by two other police officers.

Charles Sitton was rushed to the hospital, although the EMTs felt it was not a cardiac arrest but only a panic attack that caused his collapse. One of the police officers went along with him. As soon as Charles was able, he would need to be interviewed.

Officer Donovan got on the radio as soon as the paramedics took over Mr. Sitton's care. "Central–76."

"76–Central."

"I need an evidence team, forensics, a detective, and a chaplain out here. If either the lieutenant or the commander is available, they would probably be a good idea also. The plane is missing, but the Romson kid's car is here. We need to get some notifications out to be on the lookout. That is a little above my pay grade."

"Roger. On the way. Out."

Officer Donovan walked back over to the Romsons, who were still kneeling on the floor embracing each other. "Folks, I'm sorry, but we need to secure this site. We will take care of locking the door. I have people coming to investigate. I think it would be best for you to go to the station so we can talk with you. In just a few minutes, this place is going to be crawling with the press, and you don't want to be here when that happens."

James Romson looked up. "Thank you. We'll drive Charles's car over."

"Really, I think it would be better if you rode with me. You've had quite a shock, and I think it would be better if I drove you."

"All right. If you think so."

Officer Donovan led them to his patrol car and seated them in the back seat. As they drove away from the building, James could see the evidence team cordoning off the area with yellow police tape.

At the police station, Officer Donovan escorted them to an interrogation room and asked them to be seated. "You are not being arrested, but I must read you your rights before we talk. 'You have the right to remain silent. Anything you say can and will be used against you in a court of law. You have a right to an attorney. If you cannot afford an attorney, one will be appointed for you.' Do you understand this?"

James looked up at him. "Yes, I understand. Does this mean we are suspected of doing away with our son?"

"No, sir. At this time, we have to ask you some questions and try to determine where your children are, where the plane is, and where the pilot is. It is merely a formality."

"I think I understand, and I have nothing to hide; but under the circumstances, I believe it would be wise for me to have legal counsel available. Let me call Bernie Watson, our corporate counsel, and ask him to come over here. I wish also to make him available to Charles Sitton when he is able to talk with you."

CHAPTER 15

Please, Jed. Could you hold me? I miss my daddy so much."

Jed knelt on the floor in front of Lizzie and tentatively reached his arms out toward her. The last thing he needed was a crybaby to babysit! He had more than enough on his hands just to survive if it was going to take as long to be rescued as he expected it probably would. Nevertheless, he knew he had to do what was necessary for Lizzie, too. If he was going to hold a girl in his arms, this was not the way he wanted to do it.

Lizzie nearly lunged at him and wrapped both arms around his neck, and she wailed on his shoulder for a good five minutes, soaking his shirt with her tears. Without enthusiasm, Jed put his arms around her and instinctively rocked her and stroked her hair. He thought he should say something, but he had no clue what he could say to help. Of all the people to be stuck with, why did it have to be a girl and, of all girls, why her?

Finally the tears stopped, leaving Lizzie gasping in great shuddering breaths as she tried to regain her composure. With great effort, she lifted her head and looked at Jed. "I'm sorry to go to pieces on you like that. Thank you." She looked around as if looking for something.

"What do you need, Lizzie?"

"A tissue?"

Jed got up from the floor, his knees aching from the hard wood, and walked into the kitchen and got a paper towel. "I'm sorry, but you'll have to make do with a paper towel. We don't normally have tissues here."

Lizzie took the towel from him and shakily blew her nose and wiped at her eyes. "I'm not trying to be a baby, Jed, and usually I'm not. I'm sorry to be a burden to you. I'll try to carry my end of the load, honest, but I don't know what I'm doing. Please be patient with me?"

A small smile and a hand extended to help her up gave his answer. "Want to take a look around now?"

She nodded and sniffed once. "Thank you." It was a whisper.

Jed led Lizzie around the area the lodge occupied. He showed her the spring and how water was collected and piped downhill to the cabin. They walked into the woods for a short distance to a small grove of hickory trees. "Mom always wants us to gather half a bushel or so of nuts when we come up here for hunting, and we take them home. Personally, I like them better in cookies than walnuts." He noted Lizzie's eyes pool at the idea, so he quickly changed the subject and led her on further. "Here is a patch of blueberries! Of course, they won't be ripe for a while yet, but they are sure good when ripe. Sometimes, the plant managers' fishing trip is during blueberry season, and we get some. I like the wild berries better than the commercially grown ones. There are also some wild strawberries around here, but they are kind of tart."

Jed led Lizzie around a small copse of trees and came nearly face to face with a gaunt bear and her cub. The bear was about a hundred yards away, but the surprise was mutual, and they seemed much closer than they really were. Putting out a hand to hold Lizzie back, Jed whispered, "Just turn around, and go back the way we came. She won't bother us if we don't threaten her. No! Don't run!" he hissed. "Walk slowly. You can't outrun her." He waited until Lizzie was around the trees and out of sight before backing slowly away. The old she-bear stood on her hind legs, watching carefully over her yearling cub as he went.

"Whew! That could have been trouble. I'm sorry, but I wasn't paying attention like I should have been."

"I'm scared, Jed. I want to go home!"

"I know, Lizzie, but you know we can't, so we just need to deal with things as they are. We weren't in any real danger there, and turning around and walking away is the right thing to do. I've never had a problem with a bear up here. It's times we startle each other like that that have a potential for trouble. If she had seen us coming, or if I had seen her first, it would have been no problem at all. Shall we take a look on the other side of the cabin?"

"I'd rather go back if you don't mind, Jed. I'm scared of the woods."

"Okay. We can head back if you like. You'll get used to it before long, and it won't frighten you any longer." He grinned at her. "You never can tell. You might like it so much you want to move up here. I would in a heartbeat." Jed led the way back toward the lodge a different way, pointing out things as they went.

"If you go about half a mile on the other side of the lodge, you will find a thicket of blackberries that are pretty good, too. With all of the marsh areas around here and all the streams and rivers, there is plenty of moisture, so things grow well. It is just a short season. North of us, they grow a lot of potatoes, but there haven't been any planted around here."

Jed recognized Lizzie struggled with the whole situation in general. He was doing his best to keep her attention focused on things at hand and away from their situation. The problem was she was not the outdoorsy type. Finding things to keep her mind occupied was going to be difficult. There was going to be a lot of hard work for them if they were going to make it. Perhaps keeping busy would be the key. Without realizing what he was doing, Jed—by taking on the responsibility for Lizzie—was giving himself a focus to keep his mind off of his own issues.

CHAPTER 16

"S o, Mr. Romson, please walk me through everything from when the young people were determined to be missing until now," Detective Sarah Summers said. She had joined Officer Donovan in the interrogation room, making it crowded in the sparsely furnished space. James and Mary Romson sat on metal seats affixed on one side of a metal table, bolted to the floor. Officer Donovan and Detective Summers sat opposite them, and Bernie Watson, the Romsons' attorney, sat at the end on the only loose piece of furniture in the room. Though the door was not locked behind them for this interview, Mary still found the whole process intimidating.

"Okay. I arrived home at approximately eleven-thirty or eleven-forty-five. Someone caused a breakdown and a small fire at the plant, and Charles and I, even though we had taken the day off because the kids were coming home, both had to go in to make sure it was repaired promptly." He went on to detail all of the information he had from the students' arrival time up until they found the doors tampered with at the hangar.

"I was particularly unhappy with the way the sergeant treated Charles dismissively when he called, saying they were eighteen, and the police basically weren't concerned about their whereabouts."

Detective Summers broke in, "Well, yes and no. We are, of course, interested in their whereabouts if foul play is involved. But without any sign of foul play, there isn't much we can do since they are adults, even though they are still in high school and live in your home."

"Okay, detective, I can understand to a degree, but it seems to me there should be a bit more interest in their well-being. Anyway, neither Mary nor I got any sleep last night, and I don't believe Charles did either.

"We invited him over for breakfast to discuss what could be done to find the kids. It was by calling the kids in the class that we found out from Teddy Baldwin about the guy with the broken-down car."

"You said Teddy Baldwin? Do you have a number for him?"

"I'm sorry, not with me. I can get it for you, though."

"Not a problem. I'll be talking with the school and can get it from them. We'll want to talk with everyone involved with the trip anyway, but this sounds most promising."

James continued, "We then came to the PD and talked with the chief and found out the car parked on the wrong side of the road belongs to Pete Richardson, my company pilot. We went to the hangar, where we found the doorknob tampered with to keep us from opening the door. We called for assistance, and Officer Donovan here showed up. You know what happened from that point."

"And why do you suspect Mr. Richardson would have any interest in your children?" asked the detective.

"Actually, he has no interest in them directly. He came to me Thursday morning asking to speak with me privately. He then asked for a loan of twenty-five thousand dollars. I can't imagine Pete doing anything to the kids. It doesn't make sense, but perhaps I should not have been so hard-hearted."

"Tell me about Mr. Richardson. Does he have family?"

"Divorced. His ex-wife moved out of state and took their two children two years ago. He has been estranged from them since."

"Tell me about Mr. Sitton and Elizabeth. Do they get along? Was there any reason she would have not wanted to return home?"

Mary spoke up. "Absolutely not! They are very close!"

"How about the relationship between Jed and Elizabeth? Is there any romantic interest or anything going on that would cause them to go off together?"

Again Mary answered. "No, not at all. They are friendly, but they don't run in the same circles, even within such a small school."

"Would it be because of the stigma of her father working for Jed's father?"

"Not at all," James replied. "Charles and I are very good friends, and we don't have a boss-employee relationship. Charles and I served in Vietnam together, and he saved my life. There is no one I hold in higher esteem, and I would be thrilled if my son was worthy of his daughter. In fact, Charles owns a stake in Romson Industries. The kids just have different interests."

Mary tried to stifle—but could not hold back—a large yawn. Everything was catching up to her, and the adrenaline rush of finding the Bronco in the hangar and the plane missing was rapidly dissipating.

Bernie Watson noticed Mary's yawn and had also noticed James's speech dragging. He interrupted, "May I suggest we put a hold on this for the time being? As you can see, James and Mary are both dead on their feet. Perhaps we could schedule a time tomorrow to continue?"

Detective Summers was not happy with the interruption. She had noted the exhaustion and had planned to use it to her advantage. In her experience, those who were sleep deprived were not very good at covering lies, and it made interrogations much easier to have suspects at such a disadvantage. She knew, though, that Bernie could just tell them not to cooperate and she would get nothing at all. She really didn't think the Romsons were suspects, but one never ruled out anyone until one knew for sure. "All right. Shall we say eight o'clock Monday morning?"

"Noon would be better. I'm sorry," said James. "I still have a business to run. I'm not saying my business is more important than my son, but I also have a responsibility to my employees. I'll need to make some arrangements in the morning, and then I'll be able to give you whatever time you need. I just have to set things up with my management team and with Charles's assistant. How about twelve? Will twelve work okay for you? Bernie?"

"All right, I guess," said Detective Summers. "I will need your plane's N-number, plus a description of the kids and the pilot. Pictures would be very helpful also. I'll call the FBI and get them involved. With a plane involved, I'm sure state lines have been crossed."

"Bernie, can you help the detective with these things? You have all the airplane info, I know. The pictures I have on my desk and Charles has on his office wall will probably be the easiest to use. They both are their senior pictures, so they are current. Of course, I have no idea what they were wearing, but when you call the other students and the trip sponsors, you may get some info from them." James's words were slurring from exhaustion as he asked Detective Summers, "Would you be so good as to give us a ride home? We took Charles's car to the hangar."

"Officer Donovan will be happy to give you a ride home. I'm sure Charles will be staying overnight at the hospital. I would suggest you take your phone off the hook when you get home. I would also suggest you put a note on your door asking people not to disturb. Most will be meaning the best, but you need rest, not people, at this time."

CHAPTER 17

W hy don't we see if we can catch our dinner?" asked Jed as he pulled a canoe from the storage area. "This time of day is usually a good time to catch some fish."

Lizzie looked at the ground and kicked at it softly. Her shoulders were slumped, and tears pooled in her eyes. "I've never been fishing. I don't know what to do." Jed was a little concerned about Lizzie's attitude. Her demeanor was listless and lethargic, and everything about her spelled defeat.

"Hey, Lizzie, listen to me for a minute." Jed turned the canoe upside down on the ground and, taking Lizzie's hand, pulled her over to the canoe and sat her on it. He sat down next to her, still holding her hand. "I know things don't look good right now, and we both want to go home, but we can't." He looked her in the eyes, making certain he had her attention. "We could have it so much worse! At least Pete left us somewhere that I know, and we have supplies and equipment to keep us going for a long time. We can fish; there is plenty of game. We could live here even if we never were found, but we will be found! This place is too important to the company. Someone will come eventually. In the meantime, we can make the most of it, or we can feel sorry for ourselves and mope. I'm just as homesick as you are, but I need your help if we are going to do this."

Lizzie squeezed his hand and whispered back, "I'm sorry for being a baby. I'm just overwhelmed, and I want so badly to see Daddy."

"That's okay. You'll have to help me when I'm feeling down, too." Jed gave her a hopeful smile. "We'll make it."

"All right. Let's go fishing, but you have to be patient with me and teach me how." Together they picked up the canoe and carried it to the dock. Jed went back to the storage area and selected a tackle box and two life jackets.

"I can swim. I don't need a jacket," Lizzie protested.

"Wrong! I don't care how well you swim. No one goes out in a boat of any kind without some kind of floatation device. If you fall in fully clothed, no matter how well you swim, you will have trouble surviving for long without one. Besides, this lake had ice on it just a couple of weeks ago. You would not last long in the water right now before hypothermia took over, and you would drown. You never take the canoe out by yourself, and you never go without a life jacket. Clear?"

"All right. I get it." Lizzie nearly pouted but nodded her assent.

Lizzie climbed into the front of the canoe; Jed stepped into the back, pushed them away from the dock, and started paddling. Lizzie picked up her paddle and tried to help but succeeded only in splashing water.

Jed chuckled. "Here, watch how I hold the paddle and what I do." He dipped his paddle deep into the water and then slowly stroked from front to back. "See, you dip the paddle, and then pull it through, kind of like stirring cookie dough. You dip it down and then pull, instead of slapping the paddle at the water." Lizzie tried again and did better, but she had trouble keeping the paddle straight so it actually pulled rather than sliced through the water.

"That's the idea. Now you just need to get the knack of using your paddle to direct where you want to go. If you allow it to rotate in your hand, you will direct the canoe one way or the other instead of straight ahead. Some people alternate sides, stroking once on the right and then on the left to direct where they go, but the turn of your paddle blade will direct you just as easily. Let's head for the point over yonder." Jed pointed with his paddle toward a spit of land that stuck out into the lake.

Lizzie continued to try to help paddle, and she was starting to get the hang of it; but it was Jed's hard work that got them to the area he wanted.

"Paddling's a lot harder work than it looks like. I'm pooped!"

Jed grinned at Lizzie as he broke out the rods and tackle, prepared what he thought was the best lure for the time of day, and handed the rod to Lizzie. Lizzie listened carefully and watched as Jed demonstrated the proper way to cast and then retrieve the lure.

"Don't be disappointed if you don't catch anything the first few times you try," he told her. "I remember I went with Dad several times before I ever caught anything. It takes a little time to figure it out sometimes."

Lizzie made her first cast, which didn't go where she wanted it to go, so she started to real the lure back in to try again. All of a sudden there was a splash of water at the end of her line, and her rod tip bent. "Quick, reel it in! Looks like you got a good one on there!" exclaimed Jed. He grabbed the hand net as Lizzie excitedly reeled in the fish, which fought hard, but to no avail, and Jed dipped out the exhausted fish with the net. "You got a lake trout! It looks like about sixteen inches. Great job!"

Lizzie was almost bouncing in her seat with excitement. She had never tried fishing before, and now to catch a nice fish on her first cast was intoxicating. Fishing was a lot more fun than she had thought it would be.

"This one is your supper," Jed said. "You always get to eat your own first fish. I promise you'll love it." The canoe had a live well under the center seat—a Romson Industries specialty—built into all their canoes. This special feature meant any fish they caught would still be alive and fresh when they returned to land. They fished for another hour, long enough for Jed to catch two slightly smaller lake trout and for Lizzie to catch one more. "We have more than we can eat for tonight, and the smoker isn't ready yet. Why don't we head back to the lodge and have an early dinner?"

Lizzie was more than ready to head back in. Fishing was more fun than she thought it would be, but the stress of the abduction, of seeing the plane crash, and of sleeping in a strange place was catching up to her. She was very tired. Once they returned to the dock, Lizzie stood in the canoe to climb onto the dock, but in her weariness over-balanced and fell backwards into the water. It was shallow enough for her to stand, but the cold took her breath away, leaving her gasping. Jed jumped onto the dock. He dropped to his belly and extended a paddle to help her out of the water. When he drew her close enough to reach her, he extended his hand and pulled her to safety.

"Brrr!" she said, wrapping both arms around herself, shivering, and her teeth chattering.

Jed dove to the end of the dock and reached out, barely catching the canoe with the end of his paddle before it drifted out of reach. "Go to the cabin right now, and get those clothes off. Crawl into a sleeping bag! Don't waste any time. I'll be up in a couple of minutes. Be in the sleeping bag by the time I get there. We don't need to deal with hypothermia along with everything else."

Lizzie stumbled toward the lodge as Jed unloaded the fishing gear. He dragged the canoe onto the dock and carried it onto land where he overturned it to protect it from weather. Carrying the fish and tackle, Jed sprinted to the lodge. Tossing the fish and gear on an old table to clean later, he quickly entered the cabin to check on Lizzie. Somewhat frightened for her, he called out, "Hey there, Lizzie. You in the sleeping bag yet?"

"Yes, but I can't seem to get warm!"

"Okay, it will take a little time. Do you have your hair wrapped in a towel or anything?"

"No. I didn't take the time. I just wanted to get warm."

"I'll bring you one in just a minute. I'm going to start a fire in the stove and get some hot tea going. Be there in a minute." Jed shoved some tinder in the firebox of the wood cookstove and lit it. He slowly added small kindling and then larger pieces. While he waited for the fire to catch, he filled an old iron kettle with water and set it atop the stove. By now the fire was going nicely, so Jed added a couple small pieces of wood topped by a small log to hold the fire and closed the door. He adjusted the damper to get a good draw up the chimney. When he was satisfied the fire was burning well, he left it and, grabbing a towel on the way, walked to Lizzie's sleeping area. "Can I bring the towel in now?"

"Come ahead. I'm decent." Jed opened the curtain and stepped through. Lizzie popped her head out of the sleeping bag where she huddled, shivering.

"Stay wrapped up. I'll dry your hair for you and wrap it. We need to get you warmed up. I wasn't kidding about the water temperature."

"That's for sure! I've never been so cold in my life! That's the softest ice I've ever fallen on." Jed was pleased to see a glimmer of a smile.

"Yeah, the water is probably about thirty-five degrees right now. Just a few more minutes in the water and you could have died. Then where would I be? The ice hasn't been off of it more than a couple of weeks. You also learned a good lesson, I hope. Never stand up in a canoe." Jed was almost scolding. "You scared me."

"I'm sorry, Jed. I knew better, but I didn't think. It isn't quite the same as Daddy's ski-boat."

Jed finished blotting as much water from her hair as he could, then he wrapped the towel around her head. "I'll check the water and see if it's hot enough for tea. How do you drink it?"

"A little sugar, please. I'm not much of a tea drinker."

"You need something hot in you right now, and it's the best I've got."

CHAPTER 18

Charles Sitton awoke not knowing where he was. The light was bright and hurt his eyes, and he felt tubes taped to his arms. His first thought went back to when he was wounded in Vietnam and had woken up in Japan in the hospital. Something was different now, though. He felt in a haze and wasn't thinking straight.

A face appeared over his, and a voice said, "Hello, Mr. Sitton. I'm Judy, your nurse. You are at Memorial Hospital. Do you remember why you are here?"

"No." The response was more of a croak than speech.

"Let me give you a sip of water, and then I'll get the doctor in here to speak with you. Just lie back and rest. We'll be right back." She whisked out of the room and returned five minutes later with a young doctor in tow.

"Hello, Mr. Sitton. I'm Dr. Shapiro."

"Please, call me Charles."

"Okay, Charles. You were brought in by ambulance a couple of hours ago. Do you remember anything about it?"

"No. All I remember is getting to the hangar and cutting the door open, and they were gone."

"I'm sorry. Who was gone?"

"Elizabeth and Jed. Pete took them. It's all my fault. If I'd been there for her like I should have been, Pete wouldn't have gotten her."

"Who is Elizabeth? Who is Jed?"

"Elizabeth is my daughter, and Jed is my boss's son. Jed was giving Elizabeth a ride home from school."

"I see," said a puzzled Dr. Shapiro. He didn't really see, but he knew better than to pursue it any further as the police officer standing guard in the corridor made very clear to him earlier. "Well, let me settle your mind about one thing. Your heart is fine. We at first thought you had a heart attack, but it looks more like a combination of stress and exhaustion. We want to keep you here overnight for observation and to pump some fluids in you. You were also a bit dehydrated. Is there anyone you would like us to notify?"

"No. I don't have anybody but Elizabeth, and she's gone."

"Um-hmm. We'll be moving you to a room in the Cardiac Care Unit, just to be safe, in a few minutes. You are in the emergency area now. We were just waiting for you to wake up before moving you. Dr. Lambert will be in to see you first thing tomorrow morning." With that, he hustled out the door, leaving Judy to prepare Charles for moving.

CHAPTER 19

Jed stopped by Lizzie's curtain and called, "I have your tea. May I come in?"

"Sure, come ahead."

Jed parted the curtain and entered Lizzie's room. He held out a large mug of tea. "It's very hot. Drink it down as quickly as you can. Don't burn yourself, though. It will help warm you up."

A shiver shook Lizzie as she reached for the mug. "Thanks, I appreciate the way you are taking care of me."

Jed shook his head. "It's nothing. We have to take care of each other if we are going to make it up here. We don't have the luxury of being selfish. You would do the same for me anyway."

"I might, if I knew what to do. I really don't know anything about living like this. I'm afraid I won't be much help."

"You'll learn. Mostly, it's attitude. If you have the right attitude, you will adapt to any situation. You just have to be willing to adapt. We have two choices as I see it. Either we complain and moan about being stuck here, or we decide to enjoy ourselves and make the most of it. Personally,

I love it up here in the wild, and I'd spend all of my time here if I could, but it isn't for everybody."

"How do you know what to do?"

"Dad, mostly. He was a Marine scout/sniper during the Vietnam War, and he learned to move through the woods and jungle without being seen or heard. He taught me how to move in the woods when I was little. You know you have learned when you can kill a deer with a knife. I'm not good enough, but he is, or at least he used to be. He doesn't have the time to spend up here much anymore. He says he would like to retire up here, but Mom won't have anything to do with it. She doesn't mind coming up for a week or two, but she starts going stir-crazy pretty quickly."

Jed looked at Lizzie, curious. "Doesn't your dad ever talk about the Marines? I know he served with Dad in 'Nam."

"No. He won't talk about it. I've asked. He says he tries to forget, but I know he can't. I know he gets jumpy during thunderstorms and when fireworks go off." Lizzie shivered with a sudden chill.

"I understand. Most veterans won't talk much, especially the ones who spent a lot of time in action. It has way too many bad memories for them, and people who weren't there don't understand. I hate it when people make unfair judgments because they don't understand or don't care. All I've been able to get Dad to tell me has been when he's been teaching me things. I've heard him and your dad talk together and listened without asking questions. Do you know Ray Hood from the Mendota plant?"

"I know who he is, but I don't know him," Lizzie said.

"He served with them, too. In fact, the Marine Corps is where Dad picked most of his managers because he knew what they were like and what they stood for. Dad says there is no training for success like the military, especially in a combat unit, because you have to depend on the guy next to you, and you have to have the character to lead them."

Lizzie had finished her tea. "The tea really helped. I'm starting to feel like a human instead of a human Popsicle now. Thanks."

"Good. Give it a few more minutes, and then you can get dressed and come outside. I'll have the fish on the fire by then."

Jed took Lizzie's cup and walked out. He built a fire in the fire pit, and while waiting for it to produce coals to cook over, he cleaned the fish.

One nice thing about being a part of a company that produced outdoor equipment was the plethora of good equipment stocked at the cabin. It took only a few minutes to scale the fish, gut and clean them, and have them ready to broil. By the time Lizzie came out, he had set the cooking rack over the fire. The fire had burned almost down to coals, so Jed walked into the lodge and fixed coffee in an old tin coffeepot, blackened from an unknown numbers of fires. He took the pot outside and set it in the coals, then laid the fish over the coals to broil.

Lizzie watched as Jed fixed the coffee and started broiling the fish. "You'll make someone a great housewife someday if you keep that up!" Lizzie giggled.

"Nah, not much chance. I'm useless in a kitchen. Out here I can make it, though."

The aroma of fish broiling was tantalizing. Lizzie realized suddenly she was ravenous. She hadn't eaten much all day. She hadn't felt like eating before, but now the smell of fish grilling had her stomach growling and her mouth watering.

"Why don't you grab us a couple of plates, cups, and some forks? I think it would be nice to eat out here tonight."

"All right." Lizzie walked back into the lodge and returned just as Jed turned the fish over to cook on the other side. "What else do you want with it, Jed?"

"I didn't fix anything else tonight. I thought we could get by with just the fish for now. Maybe later if we are hungry we can eat something else. Mom says I'm weird, but when I've caught fresh fish and grill it like this, I don't like anything to interrupt the flavor and enjoyment. See what you think, and next time we can do it differently if you like."

Carefully, he pulled the fish from the rack and placed the large trout and the smallest one on Lizzie's plate. "You get to eat your first catch all by yourself. It's our tradition. If you don't want both you don't have to eat them, but I have an idea you will surprise yourself. Be careful of bones. I grilled them whole, instead of filleted."

Lizzie was cautious as she peeled the meat from the bones and took her first bite. "This is really good! What did you do to it? I don't usually care much for fish, but this is wonderful!"

Jed just grinned. "It's easy. Fresh fish right out of the water, cleaned, and put directly on the grill over an open hickory fire, eaten in the fresh air when you are hungry. It works every time."

CHAPTER 20

D etective Summers spent a fruitless afternoon talking with students, teachers, and sponsors, trying to find any information to help with the investigation. However, unlike on TV where the detective always finds a nugget of information from each person interviewed and is able to put a case together in a short time, life didn't work that way, and she knew it. It took hours, and sometimes days, of fruitless fact-checking, stories, and information to maybe find one little piece of evidence to use. Everyone she spoke with corroborated what James and Mary Romson had told her, which didn't surprise her. Neither of them had been real suspects from the beginning, but she never assumed anything in an investigation. Every lead had to be chased down to the end of the lead.

Each student, teacher, or sponsor had been accounted for, except for Teddy Baldwin. One would think he would want to stay home the first day after returning from Europe, but no, he had to go out of town to his grandmother's to celebrate her birthday. Detective Summers would have to follow up with him on Sunday, meaning she had to work overtime again.

Sometimes she hated her job. The idea of having time for herself away from work did not seem to fit in with her job description. Two failed marriages attested to this. It was not because Sarah had not tried. She really had, but the pressures she placed on herself and her dedication to doing her job to the best of her ability had been too much for either of her husbands to accept.

Sarah decided to call it a day—night actually—and go home and pamper herself with a nice long bubble bath.

CHAPTER 21

With supper over and the sun beginning to set, Jed doused the fire. He carefully poured water over the coals and then gently sifted through them with a stick looking for any glowing ember. Lizzie watched as he poured more water over an area he wasn't sure about. "Why are you going to all that trouble, Jed? The fire is in the fire pit. It can't go anywhere, even if it does flare up again."

"When you are out in the woods, you can never be too careful of fire. It only takes one spark to start a big fire. You always 'put a fire out after you put the fire out' is the way my dad taught me. It takes only a few minutes, and it's better than an accident. We had better get inside. The mosquitoes can get ferocious in the evenings."

Jed led the way to the lodge, carrying the coffeepot and cups. Lizzie carried in the plates and utensils. Jed drew water from the hot water tank on the cookstove for the few dishes and then refilled it. He obviously knew his way around and had done this before. Lizzie groused, "I feel so helpless. I don't know what to do to help."

"Don't worry! You'll pick up on things soon enough. Remember, I've been doing this since I was knee-high to a hoptoad."

Lizzie giggled at the expression. "My dad says that. I've never heard anyone else use the expression." Quickly, the look of pleasure washed from her face at the thought of her father.

"Hey, now. You make me feel like you don't like my company or something."

Lizzie gave him a lopsided smile. "It's not you. I just miss my dad. Europe was the longest I've ever been away from him. I don't know how he is handling all of this. He must be out of his mind."

"I know. I've been wondering about my folks, too. I decided there isn't anything I can do about them, so I'm just going to do the best I can to take care of myself and you, too, so we can get back to them."

"Do you really think we will be found?"

"I have no doubts. I just don't know how soon. This is not someplace they will think to look. They'll think Pete took us somewhere they won't know about, and, without the plane and pilot, there wouldn't be a way for them to get up here anytime soon anyway, unless they thought we were here."

"Can't they just get another plane?"

"I don't know how insurance works on this. For one thing, they don't know the plane crashed, so they will be looking for it. I don't think the insurance company will just shell out for another plane until this one is found, or at least not for quite a while. Dad bought our Beaver cheap when it was surplussed out by the government. He's made a lot of upgrades and improvements on it since then. I know he couldn't buy one like it for less than half a million, probably more. I know it will be way more than he paid for ours."

"Wow! I didn't know it was so valuable!"

"Yeah. They don't make the Beaver anymore, and it's the biggest single-engine plane. Plus, it's designed for getting in and out of places like this, so there aren't a lot of options. That's why I've been thinking long-term about staying here."

"Poor Daddy. Your parents have to be hurting, too, but they have each other. Daddy is all alone since Mom died. I've tried to get him to date, but he says he isn't interested."

CHAPTER 22

Charles Sitton awoke early Sunday morning. He was groggy from the sedative given him the night before. At first he didn't recognize where he was, but then everything came back with a rush. Tears welled in his eyes, and he felt tightness in his chest. Elizabeth! Friday had been the day he had lived for during the ten days she was in Europe. The equipment breakdown and fire at the plant had been the beginning of a nightmare. He had struggled to keep his mind on his work, wanting so badly to go home and see her, knowing she should be at home. He was so lonely since Collette died, and he had poured his whole life into Elizabeth. She kept trying to get him to date and find someone new, but he felt that doing so would betray his late wife. He missed Collette desperately, but he was slowly coming to terms with her death.

Elizabeth missing, on the other hand, was different. He felt he had abandoned her to danger because he had not been there to pick her up from the school. It was his job to protect her, and he had failed. He knew deep down that thoughts of failure were irrational, but still they were in his mind. He missed his morning hug and the "Love you, Daddy" that was his every day.

A soft knock sounded on his door, which was ajar, and it opened to a nurse pushing a cart before her. "Good morning, Charles. I'm glad to see you awake. Did you rest well?" The nurse bustled around the room, checking the monitors he had hooked up to him. "Your blood pressure, pulse, and heart rhythm all look good. Are you feeling up to a little breakfast?" She stuck a thermometer in his ear.

"I guess."

"It will be here soon. They are delivering them now. Your temperature is fine. The doctor will be in to see you shortly." She hesitated and then went on. "I probably shouldn't say this, but I want you to know I know how you feel. When my ex-husband took my son four years ago, I thought my world would end; but I got through it, and you will too. He was gone for almost a year before I got him back. I know the heartache and the loss you feel, but keep your chin up. I'm praying they will be found soon." With that, she walked out of the room, pushing her cart in front of her.

Charles's breakfast tray came in the door as she was leaving: oatmeal and stewed prunes, two food items he thoroughly detested. All he ate of the breakfast was a single piece of cold toast, and he drank the cup of lukewarm coffee. It was a lousy way to start the day. Charles knew he was a little on the grumpy side. Sedatives always left him moody.

Ever since he was wounded in Vietnam, he made it a point to take no more medication than was absolutely necessary because of all the painkillers he had been given then. The attendant addiction to pain meds had taken six months of abject misery to break. He would have refused the sedative had he been given the option. Now he had to deal with the after effects of the barbiturate. Charles detested losing control of his faculties.

A gentle knock at the door announced Doctor Lambert and the nurse. "Good morning, Mr. Sitton. I'm glad to see you awake and looking much better than last evening. I have some good news for you. After looking at your overnight charts, your blood work, and your EKG, I can assure you there was no heart attack. What we believe happened was stress-related. I understand you received a very bad shock yesterday, and I'm sorry for it. I certainly hope your daughter is found quickly and returned to you safely."

"Thank you, Doctor Lambert."

"Now, I would like you to remain here at least until this afternoon for observation, just to be on the safe side, but I don't see any long-term effects. After you are discharged this afternoon, I want you to take at least a week off work and rest. You were totally exhausted when you came in here last evening, which was a major contributing factor. You were also dehydrated. During the next week, you are to rest and be sure to drink plenty of fluids, non-alcoholic . . ."

"No problem. I don't drink."

"Good! That relieves a lot of concern for me. I didn't want you leaving here and crawling into a bottle. I will give you a prescription for sleeping tablets, and you will take them."

"I don't take drugs, doctor."

"So I understand. I admire that, and I have also been told why. I appreciate your caution, and I wish all my patients had your mindset. These tablets, however, are not habit-forming in any way, nor do they contain any opiates or narcotics. They work with your body to cause you to sleep, but they will not interfere with your thought processes. You are perfectly safe with them. Please, don't try going without them for at least the next five days, preferably ten. Your body needs the help to rest, and with all you have on your mind, I don't believe you will do so without help. I don't want to see you back here with an actual heart attack because you stressed your body and mind overmuch. Sleep will be necessary."

Doctor Lambert handed Charles his business card. "Here is my direct office number. I want to hear from you at any time, day or night, if you have any chest pains, difficulty breathing, or any other issue. You will not be a baby or a wimp if you call, but you will be a fool if you don't. Do you understand me, Staff Sergeant Sitton?"

That brought a slight smile to Charles's lips as he came as close to attention as he could lying in a hospital bed.

"Aye aye, sir! It's been an awfully long time since I was a staff sergeant, doctor."

"Good. It's been a long time since I operated on you in Tokyo General Hospital, too."

Charles sat upright in the bed with incredulity on his face. "You were at General, Doc?"

"Yes. In fact, you were the last Marine I operated on before returning stateside in March of sixty-eight. You nearly didn't make it. I normally didn't keep in touch with my patients after they left my care, but since we are in the same town and because of the severity of your wounds, I kind of watched you from a distance. I hated losing patients then, and I hate to lose them now, so I hope you will follow my instructions."

"Will do, Doc, and I want to say thank you, twice over now."

"Sue, I think you can disconnect the monitors. I see no need to continue them any longer. Leave the IV in until we discharge Charles, if you will, please." Turning to Charles again, he said, "Charles, I would suggest you listen to Sue. She has been through a similar situation, except hers was a spousal incident, but still she understands your angst. Not that it matters, but she was my chief surgical nurse in Tokyo, so she has known you longer than you have known her. You two take care of each other, you hear?" He turned and walked out the door.

Charles looked at Sue. "I guess I owe you double thanks then also. I don't understand what he meant when he said for us to take care of each other, though."

Sue's face colored. "He was just trying to be funny."

Charles looked at her with puzzlement, but Sue didn't elaborate. She knew Doctor Lambert was just trying to match-make, as he had been doing ever since her divorce. When her ex-husband had taken off with her son, she had been frantic with worry, so she was able to understand Charles's concern for his daughter. This gave her more of a connection with her patient than normal. She tried to remain professional and not let her emotions come into play, but it was impossible now. Her compassion was obvious, and Charles was appreciative.

"What is your last name, Sue?"

"Jenson. I went back to my maiden name after the divorce. It was Thompson."

"I remember. It was a tough time, I know. How is your son doing now?"

"He's doing okay. He's fourteen. He struggles at night sometimes, and if I get stuck working late, he's afraid I won't come back. Doctor Lambert and his wife have been good with him, and Doc tries hard to be a good masculine role model. Jimmy really needs someone to look up to."

"Maybe he would like to go on our fishing trip to our place up in Maine? I don't have a son to take with me like the other managers do." Then his face fell, grief stricken. "I guess that isn't going to happen now, though."

Sue was overwhelmed with compassion for her patient. She reached out and grasped Charles's hand. "That was sweet of you. I know he would love it, and you will be taking more trips. You will get your daughter back, too. Keep your hopes up." She gave his hand a squeeze and felt tears in her eyes as she saw the pain in Charles's.

Charles saw the compassion in her eyes, and he covered her hand with his other hand. "Thanks. That means more than you know." He felt a stirring in his soul he had thought he would never feel again. It wasn't much, but a glimmer of hope remained in his subconscious.

Almost reluctantly, Sue withdrew her hand. "I must see to my other patients. I'll check on you in a little bit. Use your call button if you need me." She left the room, but glanced back at Charles before she walked out the door. She felt the same stirring.

CHAPTER 23

J ed woke up early again Sunday morning and lit a fire in the cookstove. When the fire was hot, he put the coffeepot on to brew and then started mixing pancakes. He fried bacon and eggs to go along with the flapjacks, debating whether to stretch them out or to go ahead and use them up. But he reasoned they would not last long without refrigeration, even though the bacon was salt cured. He flipped the pancakes on the griddle and called out to Lizzie.

"Hey there, sleepyhead. We're burning daylight! Coffee's on and the jacks will be done in just a jiffy." He heard a groan come from Lizzie's room and knew she was moving. She stumbled out of her room a few minutes later, running her fingers through her hair. She looked unhappy.

Lizzie rubbed her eyes a time or two and said, "This hotel is really lacking on the shower facilities. I need to wash my hair. How in the world did people do it in the old days?"

"Actually, as late as 1900, women washed their hair only about once a month. That's one reason they wore it up in buns or braided it, so it didn't look so bad."

"Ugh! That's terrible!" Lizzie made a face.

"I guess you could go down and take a bath in the lake if you want. Wake you up, at least!"

"Very funny."

"Sit down and have a pancake—or five. We'll figure something out after breakfast." Jed poured her a cup of coffee and slid it in front of her. "I hope you like salt bacon. It's all the meat we have."

"It's fine. Smells good. What's with you in the mornings anyway?"

"I don't know. I've always been an early riser. Just like getting up and getting going, I guess."

"Ugh. Daddy and I have an agreement. I take care of dinner, and on the weekends I do lunch, too, but he is on his own for breakfast. I usually just get up in time to get out the door to school and eat something on the way. He always leaves me a cup of coffee in the pot when he leaves for work."

"Well, today is Sunday. We obviously aren't going to church, so I thought we would just have a little quiet time of our own and then take it easy today. We'll try to keep things as normal as we can. I think doing so will help us keep things together. What do you think?"

"Sounds good to me."

CHAPTER 24

James Romson opened his eyes to the smell of coffee and bacon. He shook the sleep from his eyes and sat up. His muscles seemed to creak as he stretched. He glanced at the clock on his bedside table and then, startled, looked again. It read one-thirty-eight in the afternoon! He had been sleeping since he arrived home from the police department at five-twenty the previous afternoon! Slowly, he rose to his feet and wandered down to the kitchen where he found his disheveled wife frying bacon and holding a large coffee cup in her hand.

"Hi, honey," he said. "You look like I feel!"

"Thanks, a lot! Remind me to compliment you sometime, too," she said as she reached her lips up for a kiss. "Good morning, darling. I think we were more tired than we thought." She started forking bacon out of the frying pan and broke eggs into the hot grease. "I know the doctor won't like the grease and cholesterol, but after a day like the last two, I'm not too worried at the moment. I thought breakfast sounded good, even if it is afternoon." James hugged her and then put bread into the toaster.

"You know, I think we might have goofed turning the phone off. What if Pete tried to reach us with a ransom demand?" James asked, as he scratched his head absentmindedly, his forehead furrowed.

"I think he will call back. I don't think that will be a problem. I looked at the answering machine, and it's full. I didn't think I could take listening to it before I had some coffee in me, though."

"Mary, I just thought of something. We didn't call either of our parents last night to tell them! I hope they didn't watch the news, but I know they were most likely swamped by people at church this morning. We'd better call them right away and apologize." He turned the telephone ringer back on and picked up the handset. After dialing his parents' home, he waited just a few moments for an answer. Mary could only hear half of the conversation, which was very full of apologies.

"Hi, Mom. James here. . . . Yes, I'm sorry we didn't call you yesterday. . . . I know, we should have thought of you. . . . No, we didn't do it on purpose. We . . . No, Mom, we were at the police department until . . . No, Mom, they didn't arrest us. . . . No, Mom, the TV people didn't talk to us. . . . No, Mom, the news people don't know what they are talking about. They . . . No, we are not suspects, and Jed was not killed. . . . We don't know. We just woke up. . . . Of course, we slept! We hadn't been to bed in . . . I know, Mom. We are worried, but . . . Is Dad there?"

Mary put the eggs and bacon on the table and buttered the now cooling toast. She handed James a cup of coffee. He waved to her to go ahead and eat, miming talking in his ear.

"Hi, Dad. Sorry we didn't call you last night, but by the time we got home from the police department, a little after five, we were totally exhausted and both fell asleep with our clothes on. I woke up not ten minutes ago. . . . No, I don't know what is going on today. I just woke up. . . . No, I don't know what the news is saying, and we have not talked with them at all. . . . No, I know they don't know anything about what happened. We are still trying to work that out. All we know is Jed picked up Pete, our pilot, when they got back from Europe and for some reason went to the hangar. His Bronco is there, but the plane is not. He had Charles's daughter, Elizabeth, with him. The lock on the hangar door had been blocked with Super Glue or something, and we had to cut the lock off the door. When we left the police had sealed the site. . . . No, Dad, the news people don't know what is going on either. The police would not have told them, and we certainly haven't talked with them. Charles was taken to the hospital with chest pains and shortness of breath. . . . No, I haven't talked with him yet either. I just now realized we hadn't called you and wanted to apologize. We didn't mean to leave you out of things; we just had too much going on to think of. . . . Yes, Dad, we'll call you right away when we hear anything. . . . Okay, Dad. Love you. We'll let you know everything we find out. Goodbye." He sat down at the table shaking his head at Mary's grin. His mother tended to be a little excitable.

Mary picked up the telephone as James started eating. She dialed her parents' number and waited for an answer. It came quickly.

"Hi, Daddy. . . . Yes, I'm sorry we didn't call you last night, and you had to hear on the news. . . . No, we really don't know what is going on. James and I had been up for almost two days, and we basically collapsed when we got home from the police department last night. . . . No, I really don't know what the news is saying happened. We just woke up about twenty-five minutes ago and realized we had not told you. . . . No, they don't have any real information. All they know is Jed and Elizabeth are missing . . . . No, we haven't talked with the police yet today. We'll be calling them just as soon as I'm through talking with you. . . . Yes, we love you too, and I'll call you just as soon as I hear anything at all. . . . Tell Mommy I love her, and I hope her migraine goes away soon. . . . Yes, I know the stress is not good for her. . . . Okay, goodbye."

Mary hung up the phone and sat down at the table with a sigh.

"Well, at least mine went a little easier than did yours." She smiled at her husband. She loved her mother-in-law dearly, but she was so glad her husband had been the one to call her.

James picked up the phone. "I suppose we'd better call the PD and see if anything new has come up, but I want to call Pastor Shepherd first before he goes to church for the evening service. I know he'll want to be able to say something about what is going on." He called the pastor's home and left a brief message telling what he knew and apologizing for not letting him know sooner. He added that he would be in touch soon and asked him to please ask folks not to call. They had more than they could handle as it was.

CHAPTER 25

etective Summers reached Teddy Baldwin Sunday afternoon just before two o'clock. She had hoped to catch him earlier, but, after church his family had all gone out to eat. They were in no hurry to get home, it seemed. She dropped by his house at three o'clock and interviewed him for over an hour, repeating questions periodically in a different manner just to be sure she was getting the right answers. He was her most important witness because he was the only one who noticed Jed stop and talk to the man with the supposedly broken-down car by the street. Though quite a number of others had noticed the car and remembered seeing it when asked, no one had recognized the car, nor had anyone else noticed a person with it. She had to be certain Teddy was telling the truth and that he was telling all of it.

"Teddy, I know we've gone over this a couple of times already, but I need to go over it one more time. I know you've told me what you saw, but I've learned in my years of police work that often, in retelling the story, a witness will mention a detail he left out earlier. It isn't intentional most of the time, especially when it is someone like you, who is trying to help me find a friend, but little items get missed in the telling. Now, can you please walk me through it one more time?"

Teddy was a little exasperated, especially since he was missing the NASCAR race at Talladega that he particularly wanted to watch on TV, but he also wanted to help find Jed and Elizabeth. "All right, we'll go through it again." Teddy sighed. "When we got back to the school, while we unloaded the bus, I heard the secretary call Jed and ask him to give Lizzie a ride home. I know Lizzie was unhappy about it because she was homesick the whole time we were in Europe. You see, she and her dad are really close since her mom died a couple of years ago. She hardly goes anywhere without him. I think it's sweet.

"Anyway, I think they were the first to leave the school. Since we got back to the school a little early, my mom was late getting there to pick me up, so I was watching the drive for her to pull in. That's the reason I saw the guy out there by his car. He pulled up just a couple of minutes after the bus pulled in and raised his hood like he had problems with the engine. I noticed he was on the no parking side of the street, but when you breakdown, you breakdown, you know?"

Detective Summers nodded her head. *So far, so good. Same story.*

"So, when Jed was pulling out of the lot, this guy waved at him, and Jed just stopped at the edge of the road. I saw the guy walk over to Jed's door, and it looked like they were talking. Nothing seemed wrong about it to me. They were just talking like they knew each other or something."

"Could you tell who it was?"

"Nah. It was just some dude."

"What did he look like? Can you describe him?"

"I dunno. I didn't really pay all that much attention to him. He was just a little taller than the top of the Bronco, so maybe about six feet? Kind of skinny. Looked like he was wearing some kind of jumpsuit or something. You know, one of those one-piece deals with a lot of pockets?"

"What color?"

"I don't really remember. Like I said, I wasn't paying much attention. Dark, maybe a blue or a gray."

"Okay, what happened then?"

"Well, the guy walked back to his car and closed the hood, got a bag out, and got in the back seat of Jed's truck."

"Did it look like he was forcing his way in, or was Jed okay with him getting in?"

"Looked like it was okay with Jed. Everything looked friendly to me."

"Did you notice what kind of car it was?"

"Yeah, it was an old Ford Thunderbird, but I'm not sure what year. I only noticed because we had one like it until last year. It was dark blue, I think."

"Did you notice the license plate, or would you recognize it if you saw it again?"

"Nah, I didn't see the plate, but I might recognize it. I'm not sure. One T-bird looks like another, you know."

"Thanks, Teddy. I appreciate you taking the time for me. I may be back in touch with you if anything comes up. Here's my card. Please, if you think of anything else, would you give me a call? I don't care what time it is, day or night. Leave me a message if I don't answer, and I'll call you back. Just tell me a good time to call, okay?"

"Yeah, sure. I hope you find them quickly. We graduate in three weeks, you know."

"I hope so, too. We are going to do our best, I promise." Detective Summers offered her hand to Teddy and left to write up her notes for her report. Everything Teddy said corroborated what she already knew but didn't leave her any closer to knowing it all. Sometimes she thought it was like putting together a jigsaw puzzle with no picture on it, and pieces were missing that had to be created to fit in. The problem was in creating the correct missing pieces so they fit together. Often, one didn't know if the pieces really fit until it was all over, and sometimes they didn't fit at all.

CHAPTER 26

Sue Jenson walked into Charles's hospital room again at three-thirty. She had been in and out several times during the day, and each time there seemed to be just a little spark of something between the two of them. After her divorce, she had decided she wanted nothing to do with men. She didn't trust them.

Oh, Doctor Lambert was okay, but theirs was a professional relationship. Sure, they had a friendship there, but it was based on work. Sue was careful to surround her son with good role models, but they were all married men, and she kept a proper distance. She didn't want to get tangled up in another abusive relationship like the one she had gotten out of. "Once burned, twice shy" is the way she described it whenever one of her friends tried to introduce her to someone.

Charles, on the other hand, had a vulnerability about him that went beyond the loss of his daughter. There just appeared to be a hole in his life. Sue knew it had to do with the loss of his wife three years earlier. Collette Sitton died just a year after Sue's divorce, and she remembered it well. One doesn't work in a hospital in a small city without knowing what goes on. Mrs. Sitton had not been her patient, but they still crossed paths frequently, and Sue observed how close Charles and his wife were. At the time, she felt jealous, almost cheated.

Charles sat on the chair next to the bed. He was fully dressed and ready to leave.

Sue grinned at him. "What's the matter, Charles? You don't like our hospitality?"

"The 'ity' part is quite fine. It's the hospital part I don't care for." He chuckled at his little joke. "I'm ready to get out of here, just as soon as the warden comes around and grants me my pardon."

Sue always tried not to get attached to her patients, keeping a professional attitude at all times, but somehow she wasn't able to do so with Charles. She reached out and laid a hand on his. "I'll be praying you find your daughter soon, Charles. I know what you're feeling. Please, if you ever need someone to talk to, give me a call."

Charles turned over his hand, catching hers in his. "Thank you, Sue. I don't remember the last time you took care of me, but I appreciate what you've done for me today. I may just take you up on your offer. My house was awfully empty with Elizabeth gone and doubly so when she didn't come home." Tears welled up in his eyes, and he dashed them away angrily with his other hand, not letting Sue's hand go.

"Don't fight the tears, Charles. You have to let it out or you will hurt yourself. I know you Marines don't cry, but forget being a Marine for a little bit and allow yourself to be a daddy. I know you love your girl, and you're a great dad. Release the pain. You can't bottle it all up."

Charles sat there with his head down and his eyes averted from Sue's. He gripped her hand almost fiercely, sharing his grief through the small but very personal contact. Sue knelt on the floor next to his chair and laid her other hand on his shoulder. Tears flowed down his cheeks, but he made no sound as he agonized over his missing daughter.

Doctor Lambert paused at the doorway, unnoticed. He quietly backed away, pulling the door nearly closed, and moved down the hallway. He recognized Charles's need for privacy to deal with his grief. He whispered a little prayer for him as he entered the next room. He could check Charles out after he saw this patient.

Sue said nothing but remained kneeling on the floor for several minutes, just allowing Charles to hold her hand while she gently stroked his shoulder. She recognized that the anguish extended well beyond just the loss of his daughter. Missing Elizabeth had opened other, long scabbed-over but unhealed wounds from years before: loss of friends and comrades and the horrors of war he had witnessed and experienced.

He was not the first combat veteran to break down and cry in front of Sue, but this time was different. She felt she participated in his grief, but not just as a medical professional. She was taking his grief on herself, and without realizing it she wept along with him.

CHAPTER 27

James Romson placed a quick call to Anh Nguyen, his secretary.

"Mr. Romson, how are you doing? And Mary. Is she okay? I am so sorry to hear about Jed and Elizabeth!"

"Hi, Anh. We are doing as well as can be expected, I suppose. I don't really know what's going on. Charles is in the hospital, but I don't think it's serious. Look, I really hate to bother you on Sunday, but would you please call all of the management team? I need them, you too, for a breakfast meeting at six o'clock tomorrow morning. Will it be a problem for you, with getting the kids off to school?"

"No, Ma can get them out the door for me. I will be pleased to make the calls for you."

"Thank you so much, Anh. You had better call Ziggy's and reserve a room. We'll meet there. Ask Ziggy to fix a buffet. I think if we try to meet at the plant, we will be interrupted and won't get things done."

"Okay, will do, Mr. Romson."

"Oh, one other thing. You'd better invite the maintenance team also. I don't know Charles's status, so we'd better prepare for his absence.

Thank you so much. I'll see you in the morning." He hung up and quickly placed another call.

"Police Department, Sergeant Donnelly speaking."

"Good afternoon, Sergeant. James Romson here. I'm trying to touch base with Officer Donovan. Could you ask him to either give me a call or stop by my house? I need to follow up with him on things."

"Stand by one." The line went silent. James waited a moment until the officer came back on the line. "Donovan said he will give you a call within the half hour, unless he gets another call."

"Thank you, Sergeant. We'll be waiting for his call."

James hung up, walked wearily to the couch, and sat next to his wife. With all the sleep he had gotten the night before, one would think he would be rested, but he felt like garbage. It seemed it took all his effort just to put one foot in front of the other. He put one arm around his wife's shoulders, and she laid her head on his shoulder. They sat in silence, each lost in their own thoughts.

When the phone rang, James jumped up to answer.

"Romsons'."

Mary hated the way he answered the phone. She said he didn't know if he was at work or at home. He always answered the same way.

"Officer Donovan here. I hope you got some good rest?" It was more of a question than a statement.

"Yes, believe it or not, we really slept. We didn't wake until one-thirty."

"Oh, I can believe it. You two were pretty tuckered out when I dropped you off. Almost thought I'd have to carry you in the house. Anyway, any chance you and your wife could meet me at the hangar? I know Charles Sitton is still at the hospital. He'll be released this afternoon, but I think it would be better if he didn't come out right now."

"Okay, we can do that. I was just waiting to hear from you before I called Charles. I wanted to be able to let him know what's going on. His car is at the hangar. How will he be getting home?"

"Not my department, sorry. If you want, you could pick him up and give him a ride home and then meet me at the hangar. Just give the Sarge a call at the station, and let him know what time you will get there. I have some reports to write up, so I'll have plenty to keep me occupied. On second thought, I'll just go over there and do my paperwork. I'll be there when you get there. If for some reason I get called out, I'll leave you a note on the door. Please don't try to enter the hangar without me."

"Very well. I'll give Charles a call and meet you in an hour or so. Thank you very much."

He closed out the call and then, looking at the number chalked on the message board, called the hospital.

"Mercy Medical Center. How may I direct your call?"

"Charles Sitton, please. I believe he is in Cardiac Care."

"One moment please."

"Hello?"

"Hey there, Charles. I hear they are going to kick your ugly old self out of there for stirring up trouble."

Mary shook her head. One would never know how much the two men thought of each other to hear them talk.

"Sounds to me like a skunk telling a possum his breath stinks. Yeah, I'll be ready to go just as soon as the doc gets in here. My car is at the hangar. Any chance you could give me a ride over there to pick it up?"

"Mary and I are walking out the door right now, and we'll be there in a jiffy. Don't be sparking up one of the nurses before we get there. We know how you are."

"Right! Like that's gonna happen. It's why I always carry a big stick with me, so I can beat them off."

James laughed. "We'll be there in just a few minutes, buddy. Stand by."

Doctor Lambert was walking into Charles's room when the elevator door opened and James and Mary stepped out. They followed him in, after asking if it was okay. They found Charles and Sue holding hands, sitting on the side of the bed talking. "Hmm, looks like you two are taking care of each other like I told you to," said the doctor.

Sue flushed, but she didn't let go of Charles's hand. "We have been talking about when Jimmy was taken by 'the-one-whose-name-will-not-be-spoken.' I was just trying to help him deal with things."

"Um-hmm. I thought you might be able to help him. Now, Charles, I don't want you going to work, to the hangar, talking with the police or anyone else about this for at least forty-eight hours. You will take the sleeping aids I prescribed for you, beginning just as soon as you return home. Is there anyone you could have stay with you for a couple of days? I'd be a lot more comfortable if you had someone available."

Mary spoke up. "Not a problem. He's coming to our house for a few days, 'til we get things sorted out."

"I think that's a good idea. Just don't discuss the situation extensively for the next two days. I want Charles to get some real rest and not to have his mind and nerves racing continuously. Do I have your word on this?"

"Yes, Doctor."

"Good. Here is my personal contact info in case you need me after hours. I want to be called immediately if anything comes up."

"James, did you know the doc here and Sue are the ones who put me back together in Tokyo General?" Charles interrupted.

"No, I didn't! Thank you! Charles wasn't a very good spotter, but he did a good job of catching grenade fragments that might have messed up my good looks."

"You caught your share of them, too, James. Charles was my last patient, but I worked on you while they were trying to stabilize Charles for surgery. I've been watching both of you, and I want you to know I'm proud of what you've done with your company. I know you've provided employment for quite a few wounded vets who wouldn't have found work otherwise. Now get out of here, and Charles, I mean it. Use those meds I gave you and rest. I don't want to see you professionally again."

"Aye aye, Doc. Thanks from all of us."

Doctor Lambert reached to shake Charles's hand but was surprised by an embrace instead. He turned away from it only to receive another from James, and then Mary, who had tears running down both cheeks.

"Thank you, Doctor. He may not be much, but he's all the husband I have. Jed would have been fatherless had it not been for you."

Doctor Lambert was visibly moved. It wasn't often he was thanked for his work so profusely and particularly not for the work he did while in the military. He nodded wordlessly, afraid his voice would crack, then turned and walked out of the room. Sue remained behind.

CHAPTER 28

Jed and Lizzie spent some quiet time together after breakfast. They didn't have a preacher, a choir, a piano, or an organ, but they opened their Bibles and spent time trying to place their thoughts someplace other than in their circumstances. It wasn't the same, but for two young people who loved God, they found it quite refreshing. This established the pattern they maintained the whole time they were at the lodge.

They spent a good bit of the afternoon going through the clothing stored at the lodge, and, as Jed had guessed, some of the clothes he had outgrown would fit Lizzie well enough. She wouldn't win any fashion prizes, but she would be clothed. Much of what was there would be too warm for summer wear, and they had a good laugh at some of the things she tried on. Jed found a few items to help stretch his wardrobe also, but he was going to be in need very soon if something didn't happen. Afterward, they pulled out some board games that were kept there for those using the lodge. All in all, they had a lazy, pleasant day, knowing it was going to get serious fast.

Jed planned to go hunting early the next morning to see if he could find a deer. It would have to be a buck because he didn't want to leave an orphan fawn that could not fend for itself. Lizzie decided to sleep in, and then she was going to try to hand wash some of their clothing from the last two weeks. Jed rigged up a couple of lines for her to hang the clothes on to dry.

CHAPTER 29

J ames and Mary got Charles settled in the guest bedroom, agreeing to stop by his house to pick up some items when Mary drove his Oldsmobile to the Romsons' home from the hangar.

When they arrived at the hangar, they found Officer Donovan waiting. Yellow crime scene tape still surrounded the building, and Officer Donovan cautioned them not to enter the building without an officer in attendance until the site was released. An evidence van was there, and a team was scouring the building and the surroundings for any evidence that might have been missed during the first inspection. Officer Donovan filled them in on what was known at this point.

"We have gone through the Bronco, Jed's, I believe?"

James nodded.

"We dusted for fingerprints, and we found three sets, two in the front and one in the back, which is consistent with what Teddy Baldwin told us. We found a scrap of cardboard in the back end, where we assume they had their luggage. It said 'Pete plane lo' and a vertical mark, and there was a broken pencil next to it. Do you have any idea what he would have been trying to say? It looked like it was written hurriedly."

James shook his head. "Sounds like he was trying to tell us something, but I have no idea what. Pete—we already know he took them, and it's obvious he took them in the plane, but I have no idea what it means. Do you, Mary?" She shook her head, puzzled.

"Okay, if you come up with any ideas, we want to hear them. I don't care how farfetched you think they are. We found some footprints over here, where the plane was parked. Two sets got into the back door of the plane, one large and one small, indicative of a male and a female, presumably Jed and Elizabeth. There was another set of prints shuffling around over the first two that look like someone supervising what the first two were doing, and then they went to the hangar door where it looks like he opened the door and pushed the plane out onto the ramp into the lake. Outside, there were a number of tracks of the same individual consistent with pre-flighting the aircraft. It appears he then started the engine and took off."

James nodded his head. "That would be the normal procedure, except we would normally board the plane outside so as to make it easier to push out of the hangar. I don't suppose Pete would want anyone to see the kids in the plane, though."

"We checked with air traffic control, but there was no flight plan filed. Is that unusual?" Officer Donovan asked.

"No, not at all. Taking off from the lake is uncontrolled, and I'm sure he was flying VFR, which would not necessitate a flight plan. Normally, we would contact air traffic control upon takeoff, just so they would know we were in their airspace, but if he stayed low until he got away from town, they probably didn't even know he was there. He could have gone anywhere from here. With the modifications we have made on the plane, he could go seven hundred fifty miles, give or take, without refueling."

"Okay, good. Good to know. We have an advisory out to all airports telling them to be on the lookout, but those can be iffy. We'll follow up to be sure they pay attention. This will give us an area of focus. Is there anything else we need to know about the plane or people?"

James shook his head. "Nothing I can think of. This just seems like a nightmare I can't wake up from. I'll need a copy of your report for my insurance company. They will want to be notified right away."

"Right. I'll have it finalized within the day. I'll leave a copy for you at the front desk if you want to stop by and pick it up tomorrow afternoon."

"Thanks, Officer. We appreciate your help very much."

"Keep your hopes up. We'll find them."

CHAPTER 30

J ed slipped out the door just as the sky was lightening in the east. He carried an old WWII military surplus M1 Garand semi-automatic rifle, 30.06 caliber, expertly worked over to make it extremely accurate. The rifle had been fitted for a scope, but Jed would not use one today. For what he was doing, he preferred to shoot over open sights. Jed was raised to revere life, and he believed to kill an animal, even for meat, without honoring it by pitting his skill against the skill of the animal was wrong. He thought hunting deer over open sights was more sporting because he had to work to get close enough to be certain of his shot. More modern hunting rifles were available to him, but he had always liked the old M1, heavy though it was.

Jed headed toward a meadow about half a mile from the lodge where there was a good chance he might find deer feeding early in the morning. To stalk them on the ground would require him to use all the woodcraft his father had taught him since he was a young child.

To see Jed working his way through the brush would have looked humorous to anyone who didn't know what he was doing. Continuously, he turned, sidestepped, and crouched, pausing and listening and timing his moves to the sounds of the breeze rustling the leaves. He knew he was not as good as his dad, but he tried. James Romson won a bet with one of his managers one year by stalking and killing a buck with a knife.

Jed frequently hunted with a bow, but today he was more concerned with getting a buck for the meat and hide. He would save the bow hunting for fun times or for when he ran short of ammunition, if they had to stay that long.

Today was a good day. As he neared the meadow, he could see several deer grazing on the new grass. He stood concealed in a small copse of trees and shrubs, certain, without even thinking, he was downwind.

Off to his left, Jed saw a black bear sow cropping grass and snuffling around small boulders. She hooked a claw under the edge of a rock and flipped it, revealing bugs, grubs, and ants, which she ate. Once she flushed a mouse, which she chased after and finally swatted with a paw before she ate it. The old bear was gaunt from a long winter's hibernation. A yearling cub by her side learned from his mother how to find delicacies beneath rocks and logs. Jed decided they were far enough away and settled down to choose which deer he wanted from the herd.

He knew deer were out of season, and he had no license, but due to the circumstances he felt it was necessary. Normally, he would follow the law to the letter and was very concerned about conservation. He understood, though, the law was for pleasure hunting, not for subsistence hunting. The Native Americans were not limited by game laws, and he felt he fit such a category. If a game warden came by to give him a fine, he would gladly pay it, for that would mean they were found!

Slipping his rifle from his shoulder where he had it slung, he adjusted the sling and crept to the edge of the brush to get a clear shot. He knelt, wrapped the sling around his arm, and took careful aim at a large buck on the far side of the meadow. He quietly slid the bolt back enough to see the brass of a cartridge in the chamber, then slid the bolt forward and bumped it with the heel of his hand to be certain it was closed. Then he raised the butt of the rifle to his shoulder again. Jed took a deep breath, let half of it out, and gently squeezed the trigger. At the crack of the shot, the meadow cleared except for Jed's buck, which leapt forward twice and tumbled to the ground.

Jed field-dressed the deer and cut out some choice cuts of meat, making a good-sized pack to carry back to the lodge. With a rope he'd brought along for the purpose, he threw an end over a tree branch and hoisted the remainder of the deer out of reach of the old bear and any coyotes that would try to get to it. The whole deer was just too much for him to carry in one trip. He would bring Lizzie back with him for the rest.

CHAPTER 31

J ames Romson sat in Ziggy's Restaurant at five-thirty Monday morning, well before the rest of his management team was expected to arrive. He needed the time to put his thoughts in order before the meeting. Ziggy, a friend of his from way back, knew him well and set a coffee carafe on the table after greeting him with a hug, without words telling him how sorry he was to hear the news. While James was appreciative of the concern and care shown, he was also embarrassed by the attention. He *knew* Jed and Elizabeth would soon be recovered and would not bear the thought of their deaths. Therefore, his thoughts and focus were totally on doing all he could to find them while maintaining as normal a life as possible.

Anh Nguyen, James's longtime secretary, swept into the restaurant to find her boss already at a table drinking coffee. "Why is it I never beat you to work? I wanted to be here before you!"

James just laughed. "Come on, Anh. I keep telling you, you don't have to be here first."

The cultural differences had been a challenge in the early days after James sponsored the Nguyen family to immigrate to the USA, shortly after the fall of Saigon. Anh's husband, Tran, had been one of the ARVN, or the Army of the Republic of Vietnam, soldiers who worked closely with James's Force Recon team, and his escape from Vietnam had been harrowing. Tran was fortunate. He had been able to bring out his wife and mother-in-law, although he lost his eldest son.

Anh, who spoke some English, had immediately become James's secretary, working closely with Mary in the early days of the company until her English improved enough to function on her own. Her devotion to her job and to James was second only to her devotion to her husband. She revered James to the point she would never call him by his first name, no matter how many times James told her to. Anh felt firmly it was her responsibility to care for all of James's needs at work, and she felt shame that she was not at the restaurant first to ascertain all was prepared properly.

Tran, who served Romson Industries as a roving manager overseeing all of the plants, followed his wife into the restaurant. He walked over to James and embraced him. "I am so sorry, my friend. Let me find this so-and-so who took them. I will get them back for you!"

James shook his head. "We have to leave it to the police, Tran. We aren't in the Mekong any longer." He remembered all too well how fiercely Tran had fought and how loyal he was to those he respected. "One other thing you can do for me is to see if you can find out who caused the breakdown and fire that morning."

Tran's respect for James had escalated almost to reverence. There was no way he could be turned loose on Pete, or whoever else was involved. "I really appreciate your care, my friend. There is no one I would rather have with me in this. Your thoughts will be very important in figuring this thing out, I'm sure."

Other members of the management and maintenance teams trickled in, each shaking James's hand and expressing their sympathies and thoughts.

Ziggy, his care and concern evident in that he himself served them, finalized preparations for the buffet, and James called everyone to order.

"I appreciate you all making arrangements to be here so early this morning. I'm sorry it was last minute, but I didn't control the circumstances." James paused for a deep breath. "Things will be confused over the next few days, and Charles and I will be absent more than we would care to be, but first things are first. In my absence, I'm appointing Tran as interim head honcho."

He turned to Tom Russell, his number two man at the main plant.

"Tom, this is not a negative reflection on you. You will take charge of the main plant in my absence, but I want Tran to head things up due to his knowledge of the other operations. These changes, at least in part, may or may not be permanent."

Tom nodded his understanding.

"Tran has had some ideas that we've discussed. He has wanted to implement them for some time now, and he has the authorization to make whatever changes he feels are appropriate. I will be in and out, as will Charles, but both of us will have other things on our minds, and we don't know how available we will be.

"Charles will not be in for the next few days at all. He collapsed with chest pains and difficulty breathing Saturday, and, after checking him over pretty well, Doctor Lambert believes it was just stress, dehydration, and exhaustion. He has put Charles on rest for a couple of days. He is staying at my home until the doctor turns him loose."

James turned to Steve Phillips, one of the lead maintenance men.

"Steve, you will be moving up to cover Charles's duties until further notice. This may or may not turn into a permanent promotion. Charles and I have discussed this and feel you can do the job, and we may be moving Charles into a different capacity. For the next couple of days, you may call on Tran or me with any questions. Please don't bother Charles. If you call him, he will be right down here, whether he should be or not, and I have every confidence you can do the job."

Steve nodded. "Thanks."

James went on to discuss general operations for the next few minutes, making clear what he wanted to be done during his frequent absences, until he was certain each person understood his increased responsibilities.

Finally, James turned to Anh. "Anh, I know you have always wanted to tell Tran what to do and boss him around like you do me. Now is your chance."

This brought a good laugh from everyone.

"I don't know anyone I would rather have covering for me than you two. Take good care of Tom, also. He will need to lean on you for quite a few things while he is getting a handle on things. I know he can handle the job; just be his backup. Now, let's all get to work. I need to go out to the plant and address the crew, then I have to meet with the detective working on this case. Thanks again for coming in this early."

Everyone trooped out quietly, with a few hugs and murmured thoughts from some of the staff, even from Anh, who had never before expressed her thoughts so emotionally. Last of all, Tran embraced James. "Fear not, my friend. We will care for your business as if it were our own, Anh and I. You go and get your children back."

CHAPTER 32

Charles Sitton awoke later than usual. The sleep aid had done its job. Initially, he was disoriented, not recognizing his surroundings; then everything came back to him in a rush. He was in James and Mary's guest room. Throwing back the sheets, he swung his feet out and sat on the edge of the bed for a few minutes, trying to get his thoughts together. Donning a robe, he wandered toward the kitchen to find the coffee he smelled.

Mary had just put the last of her breakfast things in the dishwasher when Charles stuck his head in the door. "Any coffee left?"

"Oh, hi, Charles. Good morning to you." Mary grabbed a cup from the cabinet and poured coffee. "Sleep well? We tried to be quiet this morning and let you sleep in."

"I don't know if I did or not. I crawled in the bed and just now woke up. I don't know what I'm going to do with myself for two days. I'm not much of a reader, and I hate watching TV."

"You are welcome to any movies we have. I don't know a whole lot more to suggest. I think the doctor just wants you to take your mind off of things and rest."

"I know. Movies bore me, and I'm not much of one for 'resting.' I rest better when I'm doing something productive. I know James isn't much of a handyman, so if you have any projects, let me at them. I promise I'll not work too hard, and it will keep my mind occupied."

"I guess I don't see a problem with that. There are a few things James has been putting off. . ."

CHAPTER 33

I t was chilly early in the morning when Jed hiked with Lizzie from the lodge to the meadow to retrieve the buck. The grass, wet with dew, drenched their legs from the knees down. Lizzie gasped when she saw a black figure vanish into the woods as they entered the meadow. It had been under the deer, leaping unsuccessfully to reach it before Jed and Lizzie frightened the creature away.

"I thought you said there were no wolves in Maine! What was that animal?" Lizzie's voice quivered.

"It looked like a dog to me. There are no wolves. There haven't been any in Maine for years. Some people want to re-introduce them, but they haven't been able to. There's just too much opposition."

Jed untied the rope holding the deer and lowered it. He didn't tell Lizzie, but he watched carefully to see if the creature would reappear. Jed knew wolves were not supposed to be in the area, but there were no people around either. So where would a dog come from?

Using a couple of short pieces of rope, Jed tied the forefeet together and did the same with the hind legs. He then threaded a pole between the legs so they could carry the deer between them. He took a towel from his backpack and folded it carefully to make a pad and placed it on Lizzie's shoulder, and then he showed her how to lift without hurting herself. "We'll take it easy going back. Just say when you need a break, and we'll stop."

It was on their second rest stop that Lizzie saw movement in the trees. "Jed! There it is again!"

Jed quickly unslung the rifle from his back then set the butt down on the ground. "It's okay. Looks like John Johnson's Labrador Retriever that got lost. I wonder how it survived the winter last year. You don't know John, do you?"

Lizzie shook her head.

"John is from our Greenville plant. He brought his dog up with him last fall to train him for duck and goose hunting. The problem was he had never shot a gun around the dog before, and the first time he shot, the dog got scared and ran away. We weren't able to find him. I'll have to give John a call and let him know we found his dog."

Jed's shoulders drooped. "Oh, yeah. I guess I won't call him either, will I?"

After slinging his rifle on his back again, Jed picked up his end of the pole. "We'd better get moving. If we sit too long we'll stiffen up, and it will be twice as hard to get moving again. I have an idea the dog will trail along with us. Maybe we can get him to follow us to the lodge."

Though the dog trailed them as they finished the trek back to the lodge, it would not come out of the woods, despite frequent calls.

At the lodge, Jed had Lizzie help him hoist the deer onto an outside table so he could butcher it. He sliced a couple of nice steaks and suspended them over an open fire in the fire pit to broil while he cut up the rest of the deer. The hike out to the meadow so early in the morning and then the trek back carrying the deer made him think he could eat the whole thing at once!

After eating, Jed taught Lizzie how to scrape the inside of the deerskin to get all of the meat and fat residue from the skin.

"You know, Jed, I should be grossed-out by this, but it's kind of fun, you know? I had no idea about butchering or tanning hides."

"I always thought so. Mom hates it. She doesn't mind cooking the meat or eating it, but she hates anything to do with butchering game. I'm glad you are willing to help. I don't think I could do it all alone."

Lizzie was pleased at the comment and gave Jed a smile. "I feel so helpless up here. I want to do all I can to help. Just tell me what to do, okay?"

"That's good! In the Indian villages, it is always the squaw's job to chew the hide to make it soft and pliable. I'll let you do that."

"Yuck! Now that *is* gross!"

Jed laughed and pointed to a log extending from the corner of the lodge. "We'll beat and stretch it soft over there. I'll teach you how we do that, unless you *want* to chew it."

Lizzie threw a little piece of fat at him and stuck out her tongue. With an inward sigh of relief, Jed realized Lizzie was coping with their situation. He decided to wait until the hide was soaked to scrape the hair side. Wet-scraping seemed to be the easier way to go for Lizzie.

While Lizzie carefully scraped the deer hide, Jed took care of the meat. He cut out as much as he thought they could use before it spoiled, and then he began the process of making jerky to preserve the rest. He carefully cut away any fatty portions and scraps and threw them toward the trees where he had seen the dog skulking in the shadows. The dog pounced on the scraps ravenously but would not come close.

Once the meat was sliced into thin strips, Jed and Lizzie worked together to marinate the meat with spices and salt in preparation for drying. Once, Jed noticed Lizzie was humming as she worked.

When scraping was finished, Jed filled an old hollow oak stump with water and put the hide in to soak and start the tanning process. The tannins from the oak would begin tanning the hide and would loosen the skin to ease hair removal.

After the meat soaked in the marinade for a few hours, Jed laid the meat on racks he suspended over a very low fire, built with wet hickory chips, which smoked, dried, and flavored the meat.

Before the day was over, Lizzie had a much deeper appreciation for the work required by the women who had pioneered the country. Her back and shoulders ached from scraping the hide, and her hands cramped from holding the scraper and slicing meat. Her skin was shriveled from being damp for so long. She knew she was going to be very ready when bedtime came, but the exhaustion was satisfying when she saw all of the meat piled for smoking. She and Jed would trade off getting up during the night to be sure the fire in the fire pit was burning properly so the meat would be well-preserved and unscorched.

CHAPTER 34

Mary met James at Romson Industries for the ride to the police department to meet with Detective Summers. There was a pronounced sense of foreboding clouding Mary's mind as they drove.

Officer Donovan was waiting for them when they walked in the front door, and Bernie Watson entered moments later from the back. Together, the four walked behind the front desk and down the hallway to a conference room. Detective Summers, who had rather sunken, bloodshot eyes, was sitting at the end of the table with stacks of papers spread before her. She cradled a large cup of coffee in her hands as if it was the only source of energy she had left.

"Please help yourself to a cup of coffee or some water if you care for any. Pardon me for not getting up, but it's been a long couple of nights."

Bernie poured them each a cup of coffee and raised an eyebrow in question to Officer Donovan, who nodded his thanks. After Bernie poured it for him, they all sat down at the table.

"I hope you don't mind meeting in a conference room instead of an interrogation room?" said Detective Summers with a tired smile. Mary smiled her gratitude.

"We were setting the stage Saturday. I didn't really suspect you of anything, but we never rule anyone out, and finding oneself in unsettling conditions often brings out things we would not normally get otherwise. Have you seen the papers or listened to the news at all?"

"No, we basically slept and rested all day Sunday, and then I was busy rearranging staffing so I could be free for whatever is needed," said James.

"It's just as well. Things should start to settle down now. How is Charles? Will he be able to talk with me soon?"

Mary answered, "I think the doctor will be okay with it tomorrow. When I left the house, he was doing some little odd jobs for me to keep from climbing the walls."

James looked at her questioningly, but she shook her head to forestall any questions.

"May I stop by in the morning, then?"

Mary answered again. "Certainly. Eleven? He sees the doctor at nine-thirty. I think we will have him stay with us for a few days at least."

"Good. Now, our status. I have talked with everyone at the school, and they have all confirmed what we talked about on Saturday. We have a description of Pete, Jed, and Elizabeth out on the wires to all law enforcement offices, plus we have called in the FBI. You may or may not hear from them. We have sent alerts to all FBOs and marinas where they might stop for fuel, but we have heard nothing as of yet. I spent most of the last two nights on this."

Detective Summers paused to sip at her coffee. "The chief is very interested in this case, and my phone has been ringing nonstop. This is the first possible kidnapping, other than family related, we have had here in almost a hundred years."

"You say 'possible' kidnapping? What do you mean 'possible'?" asked James indignantly.

"We cannot characterize it as a kidnapping because there is no conclusive evidence of force being used. We have to characterize it as a possible kidnapping until we know for sure. What we have is two missing teenagers; a missing, possibly stolen airplane; a missing pilot; and some vandalism to the doors at your hangar. At present, we have to treat it as grand theft of an aircraft, with Jed and Pete as persons of interest in the matter."

"What?" James almost shouted. "What do you mean calling Jed a person of interest? He didn't steal the airplane. Surely you aren't calling him a suspect!"

"Easy, James," interjected Bernie. "She didn't call him a suspect. A person of interest is someone the police wish to talk to concerning a matter. It sounds worse than it is."

"Okay," said James, only partially mollified. "Do you mean he will be arrested?"

Bernie answered, "No. He may be detained for questioning but not arrested, at least not without reason to believe he was complicit in the theft of the airplane."

Detective Summers broke back in. "James, Mary, you need to consider what we know and what we don't. First, we have two missing teenagers who may have run off together, possibly with the complicity of a pilot." She held up her hand to stop James and Mary's outbursts. "I have to look at possibilities, not what I want to think. I'm sorry, but I don't have the luxury of emotion. I have to look at things as they are, not as I want them to be."

Mary nodded, with tears welling up in her eyes. "We are assuming because the car was left in the hangar and because a person driving Pete's car was picked up by Jed, they all left in the plane. Assumptions are dangerous in police work, but it's what we've got. Second, we have two missing teenagers who may have been taken against their will for reasons unknown. Were they taken for spite? For ransom? Or did something worse happen? We don't know, and in police work 'we don't know' means we don't know. Third, we have a missing aircraft and pilot. Appearances from footprints in the hangar indicate, but are not conclusive, that three people boarded the aircraft. This could have been for a joyride. Perhaps Jed just wanted to give Elizabeth a plane ride, and they had trouble and had to put down somewhere. However, only one set of footprints appears to be from someone pushing the aircraft out of the hangar. There is one other possibility I have been looking into for the last two nights."

Detective Summers looked through a pile of paperwork on her desk, extracted a sheet, and rubbed her eyes before looking up.

"Three small planes crashed within three hundred miles over the weekend. Although I had the incident reports from local authorities, I have been to each of the crash sites. I can say none of the three were yours, but I had to check. No other light plane incidents have been reported anywhere in the country.

"I checked with the FBI, and there have been no reports of your plane refueling anywhere within a thousand miles of here, which is well outside of your plane's range, which could indicate they are within that area."

James rose shakily from his seat and walked over to the coffeepot and poured himself another cup.

"Anyone else for a refill?" No one responded, and he took his seat.

"Okay, there is one more factor we have to consider. There has been no ransom demand, has there?"

The color drained from both James's and Mary's faces as they shook their heads. Neither of them had even considered a ransom call, or the lack of one. This put a whole new spin on things.

CHAPTER 35

Charles answered the phone on the third ring, as he knew James did. "Romsons'."

"Hello. This is Sue Jenson. I'm looking for Charles Sitton."

"Oh. Hi, Sue, this is Charles." He felt a little flutter in his stomach at the sound of her voice.

"Doctor Lambert wanted me to give you a call and see how you feel today."

She didn't mention she was the one who suggested the call. Doctor Lambert noted the connection between them in the hospital room and felt the contact would be good for both parties. Had he not specialized in cardiology, psychology would have been the field of choice. He was also a hopeless romantic.

"I'm doing well. I slept until almost ten o'clock. You have to let me go back to working, though. I can't stand being cooped up like this. I've already fixed all the things around the house James hasn't gotten around to fixing. I'm pacing around like a caged tiger. If I don't have something to do, my mind keeps thinking."

Sue laughed. "Doctor Lambert told me almost exactly what you would say. He didn't know you would be doing things around the house for James, though. You don't have any chest discomfort? Any shortness of breath?"

"No. Everything is fine. I think I just was exhausted and overwhelmed. I'm fit as a horse!"

"Okay, good. The doctor said it would be all right for you to go back to work tomorrow if, and it is a big if, you take it easy. I don't want you—I mean—the doctor doesn't want you to overdo yourself. If you feel the first sign of chest discomfort or shortness of breath, you are to call the office immediately. Understood?"

"Sure. Thanks a lot."

"You are to continue taking the sleep aids, though. Don't quit taking them without checking with us first. You need to get your rest, and at night, when things are quiet, is when the mind tends to wander. They will really help you—I know."

"Okay. I'll keep taking them. Look, you said if I needed to talk about things you were available. Could we get together and talk sometime soon?"

"Certainly. When would you like to talk?"

"How about this evening? Could I pick you up after work and take you to dinner? Just someplace quiet so we can talk?"

"Actually, I'm just leaving the office now, but I have to go pick up my son."

"Great! I'll meet you there in about ten minutes, and we can pick him up and take him with us, if it's okay with you."

Charles threw on a clean shirt, scribbled a short note to the Romsons, and hurried to his car. He felt almost like a schoolboy. As Charles raced to the hospital, guilt suddenly hit him. How could he be happy while Elizabeth was missing?

CHAPTER 36

For Jed and Lizzie, June and July, with their long hot days, seemed to pass in a blur of constant work to survive. Much of the newness wore off for Lizzie, and she developed a routine for the day tending to the smoker, fishing with Jed, occasionally going out into the woods and meadows with him to carry back a deer, and learning to use the wood cookstove—although because of the heat, she saved using the stove for rainy days when she couldn't cook outside. Much of the work was boring and repetitive, and she was alone in the lodge. The time spent fishing with Jed or going out to retrieve a deer became the highlight of her days.

Lizzie also began carrying any meat scraps to a spot halfway between the lodge and the woods for the dog. "Come and get it. You don't have to be afraid. Let me pet you," she would say softly whenever she saw the dog. He seemed to want to be close, but he would never come to her for the scraps, nor would he allow either her or Jed to approach. Instead, he would skulk over to the scraps and gobble them down as soon as Lizzie walked back to the cooking area.

A number of times when she walked with Jed to pick up a deer, she could see the dog trailing them among the trees as if happy to be close to people but still retaining his freedom. "Come on and walk with us," she would call out to the dog, but he kept his distance.

It didn't take long for Lizzie to understand why women in the early 1900s and before didn't wash their hair frequently! Carrying hot water in a bucket into their little bathroom and trying to bathe in the little tub was a lot of work, but pride forced her to try to keep herself looking nice, even though there was no one but Jed to notice, and she found she wanted him to notice. Jed pointed out one big difference to her one day when she complained about how hard it was.

"At least you have a tub with a drain in it. In the old days, they had to carry the water outside to dump it, too." His smirk was infuriating.

Lizzie did try bathing in the water coming from the spring once, but it was just too cold.

It was only in the still of the night that she struggled with homesickness, and an occasional tear would trickle down her cheek. As hard as they worked during the day, she rarely lay awake long enough to get homesick.

Jed, on the other hand, loved every second of it. Of course, he missed his parents and friends, but the outdoor life, though hard, was enjoyable.

Three months had now passed. Jed and Lizzie settled into a routine that kept them busy from waking until dark, which came earlier each evening. No longer did they talk about when they would be found. It seemed all they knew was the daily struggle to provide and survive. Life, though, was not without its enjoyments.

Jed entered the cabin carrying a buckskin shoulder bag made of remnants from making Lizzie's outfit. She found her buckskin outfit to be durable and quite comfortable once she became accustomed to it. Jed was wearing a similar outfit, but he had to wait a while before making his, as he had to kill and dress the hides of two small bucks. Once he showed Lizzie how to cut and stitch together her outfit using sinews from the deer for thread, she used a pair of his trousers as a pattern and made his pants. The shirt was easier. He cut a hole in the middle for his head, and then Lizzie marked where to cut it for seams on the sides and for sleeves. It wouldn't be featured in any fashion magazines, but it was comfortable and functional.

The supplies Pete had left in the lodge were nearly depleted and were used sparingly. Lizzie tried to keep them for something special, and they lived as much as possible off the land. Fish had been relatively abundant, and there was a good supply of dried and smoked fish in the lodge. Jerky had been set aside also.

Jed kept an eye out for edible plants and herbs when he was out, and Lizzie had learned to find edible plants as well. Cattail grew in abundance close by, and from a survival cookbook Lizzie found in the lodge, she learned to roast the tubers and even to make a sort of flour from them, although it was difficult and time consuming.

Lizzie adapted well to cooking and even enjoyed it. There were a variety of recipes in the survival cookbook for various game animals, plus it showed her how to make flour not only from cattail tubers, but also from acorns; how to find edible, nutritious roots; and how to find wild herbs and plants, which could be used as seasonings. Turtle soup was her favorite dish.

She had to admit skunk was not too bad. Initially she rebelled, but Jed said it had already sprayed him, so they might as well use it. Lizzie refused to cook the skunk, so Jed made a stew with some wild onion, wild garlic, wild rice, and cattail pollen. If she hadn't known what it was, she really would have liked it.

Jed, of course, smelled for a week!

Fat was their biggest problem. It seemed they were always hungry because the meat was so lean. Both had lost weight, leaving them lean and strong, but Jed was worried, knowing they needed more fat if they were going to survive winter.

CHAPTER 37

J ames and Mary Romson struggled through each day, trying to maintain a normalcy to their routines, always hoping for some word of Jed. Each day widened the gulf between their memories and their newfound reality. Every other day or so, James touched base with Chief Washington, but of course there was no news to be had.

Charles's grief was obvious. At work, he went through the motions, but his heart was not in it. His life's only bright spot was his growing attachment to Sue Jenson. Sue's experience, plus her warmth of heart, gave him something to hold onto. Charles looked forward to having dinner with her and her son, Jimmy, a couple of times a week.

His house no longer seemed like a home but a prison where he was locked away with the memories of his deceased wife and missing daughter. He dreaded going home at night to an empty house that had once been a haven when he was released from the Marine Corps. Now it was just an empty shell where he found himself staring at pictures of Collette and Elizabeth while tears dripped onto, and drenched, his shirt.

James and Mary did their best to include him at dinner and other activities, but he felt he was imposing on their grief.

Detective Summers was frustrated. In three months there had been no news, nor any new clues, to give her direction in her search. She had other crimes to deal with but found herself going back over this case at night during her off time. Baffled by the impasse, she tried to balance it with her other work, but this case captivated her.

CHAPTER 38

Jed emptied his bag into a large bowl on the table. He had picked two quarts of blueberries, which brought a squeal of delight from Lizzie. "I also found a bunch of blackberries. They are really early. Blackberries usually don't get ripe until later in August. We will need to take some buckets to pick them, though. They would be ruined if I put them in the bag. Some of the blueberries got squashed as it is."

Lizzie was excited. "Let's take a lunch with us and both go picking tomorrow! I would love to have some blackberries, too."

"Okay. I had hoped to shoot another buck today, but I didn't see any. All I found were does, and it's still too early for them. Their fawns would probably make it alone, but I don't want to leave an orphan that can't survive.

"I did see tracks of a moose, though. From the size of the tracks, it probably weighs nine hundred pounds or so. Don't really think I want to try dragging one of them home. Anyway, that's how I found the berries."

Lizzie dipped her hand into the bowl of blueberries and popped half a dozen into her mouth. She savored the flavor and sweetness. Their sugar had run out over a month ago, except for a very small amount she had saved, and the sweet blueberry taste was welcome. Jed smiled at her delight, but he had been eating berries as he picked them, so his sweet tooth was somewhat satiated. Lizzie was so easy to please. He thought how lucky he was to be stuck there with her, if he had to be stuck with anyone. He quickly quashed those feelings. This was not the time or place to start getting mushy about a girl.

"I found a bee tree today, too. I think there is a smoke pot and bellows around here somewhere. If I can find them, we'll get some honey."

"Aren't you afraid of being stung?"

"If I smoke them right, we shouldn't. I've watched Dad do it a couple of times, though I've not tried it myself. Be nice to have something to sweeten things with. Let's get some berries tomorrow, and we'll see about the honey later."

"Thanks for bringing me the berries. I've been craving something sweet. I found a recipe I hope you like. I thought something different would be good."

"Sounds good. What is it?"

"It's a fish chowder. I found some wild rice in that little cove south of us, and I used it in the chowder. I've got to admit I was a bad girl, though. I took the canoe down there by myself to harvest the rice."

Jed started to get angry, and his face flushed.

"I was careful, Jed. I've learned how to handle the canoe, and I wore the life jacket. The water isn't cold like it was when I fell in before. I didn't go out into the lake but stayed right by the shore."

"It's still dangerous. What would I do if you drowned? Did you think about that?"

"Sure, but what about when you go out in the woods all by yourself? What if something happens to you? Don't you think I worry about that sometimes?"

"I've been doing this since I was a little kid, though. You don't know what you are doing out there."

"Well, thank you! I've been paying attention to what you've taught me, and I've learned how to handle the canoe, plus I read how to harvest the wild rice in a couple of the books here. I think I can take care of myself sometimes. Do you think I want to just stay in the cabin all the time and eat the same old things over and over when there are other things out there if I'll just go get them? Do you think I'm just a helpless baby?" Lizzie jumped up from the table and ran back to her area and closed the curtain behind her. She only wished she had a door she could slam.

Jed watched her stomp away and then shook his head, puzzled, before walking out the door to work on treating his latest hide.

CHAPTER 39

J ames Romson resisted the urge to slam down his telephone receiver. Thirty minutes had been wasted arguing with his insurance adjuster over the replacement of Romson Industries' aircraft. Although it had been ninety plus days since Jed, Lizzie, and Pete had disappeared, along with his airplane, the insurance company dragged its feet. Their excuse was the possibility of his son being complicit in theft of the aircraft, with the implication that James himself was culpable in a conspiracy.

Although not nearly as nice as the former plane, James found another Beaver available for purchase, but without the insurance money, he didn't have the funds. His banker wasn't willing to loan enough to purchase the new plane outright, even on the proviso the insurance would eventually come through. The banker was very apologetic, of course, and blamed the loan committee for their refusal. What it all boiled down to was simple: Romson Industries was grounded.

Finding a qualified company pilot also proved difficult. Most qualified bush pilots wanted nothing to do with flying from town to town in civilized areas, and few who liked corporate type flying were interested in a propeller-driven aircraft or flying into wilderness areas. The annual goose hunting trip, scheduled for the first and second week in September, had to be cancelled. It was unfortunate because the hunting trip was always a good outreach to buyers from some of the larger sporting goods companies. James checked commercial airline rates, but tickets for two would be as expensive as flying six in the Beaver, plus he would have to lease a float plane and local pilot to ferry them from Presque Isle to the lodge. Flying them to the lodge in a smaller aircraft was just not feasible, and leasing a Beaver and pilot for the time necessary was too expensive.

CHAPTER 40

Sue Jenson was busy preparing a dinner of hot dogs and mac and cheese for herself and Jimmy when the doorbell rang. Although it wasn't late, she did not expect visitors. It was probably one of Jimmy's friends. Her day had been difficult at work. One of her patients died, and no matter how long she had been nursing, it still hurt to lose a patient, especially a young mother, as this one had been.

She had come home from work and changed into an old pair of jeans with a knee out and a paint-spattered T-shirt. She wanted comfort, not to impress anyone. She called out to her son, "Jimmy, get the door."

She was stirring the cheese sauce into the macaroni when a voice startled her, causing her to flip the spoon into the air and onto the front of her shirt.

"Well, hey there. Dressing to impress, I see!"

She spun around to see Charles Sitton standing in her kitchen doorway, grinning from ear to ear.

"What are you doing here?" she asked, almost annoyed. She really couldn't be annoyed with Charles. She had grown quite fond of him and enjoyed the times they had spent together the last few weeks. "I wasn't expecting anyone."

She swept her hand over herself, indicating her attire. Her hair was disheveled since she hadn't even bothered to straighten it after changing clothes. After all, she thought it was going to be just her and Jimmy and a quiet evening trying to get work out of her mind.

Charles chuckled. "I kind of gathered that. Jimmy let me in and said you were in the kitchen. You know, I kind of like you this way. You look real." He flushed as he realized how that could have sounded. "I like you dressed up, too! Don't get me wrong."

Sue dabbed at the cheese sauce on her shirt, ineffectively, with her attention on Charles more than on the cheese.

"Is something wrong? Did you need something?"

The grin on his face faded, and his eyes misted over.

"I just realized it has been three months today since Elizabeth went missing, and I couldn't stand being in the house alone. I didn't know anywhere else to go where I wouldn't be alone in a crowd, so I thought I'd drop in on you and see if you would like to grab some dinner. I really don't want to eat; I just don't want to be alone, and . . . and . . . well, I just don't have anyone else." Charles realized he was rambling, but he couldn't seem to stop.

Sue sensed his thoughts. Without even thinking, she stepped to the doorway, wrapped her arms around Charles, pulling his head down onto her shoulder, and held him to comfort him. She remembered only too well the feeling of loss when Jimmy was taken away from her. Charles was such a dear, sweet man.

Suddenly, Sue realized she was holding the spoon in his hair, and cheese sauce was dripping from the spoon down the open collar of Charles's shirt. She drew back, horrified, and saw cheese smeared on the front of his shirt, from her shirt.

Her hand flew to her mouth as she exclaimed, "Oh, my goodness! I'm so sorry! Look what I've done to your shirt."

Charles was trying unsuccessfully to dig cheese sauce from the inside of his shirt collar where it stuck to his skin. He grinned. "If you didn't want me to come over you could have said so. You didn't have to be so 'saucy' about it."

He chuckled at his pun, but Sue looked at him, confused. She didn't know what he found so funny, but she wasn't going to worry about it.

Quickly dampening a paper towel, she said, "Turn around, and let me see about the sauce in your collar."

She couldn't get to all of it, so Charles slipped off his shirt. Some had gotten onto his T-shirt, but Sue was able to wipe most of it off. "Let me throw your shirt into the washer before it dries and stains. You'd better see about the cheese in your hair."

Jimmy came strolling into the kitchen. "Hey, Mom. What's burning?"

"Oh, no!" wailed Sue as she snatched the broiler door open to find blackened, shriveled-up hotdogs.

Charles laughed, walked over to the wall phone, and from memory called and ordered a pizza.

CHAPTER 41

Jed and Lizzie left at first light, each of them carrying buckets. The argument of the night before weighed on their minds but was left unspoken.

The air was brisk, causing Jed to think of the coming of fall and all he needed to accomplish before winter.

After walking quite some distance in silence, Lizzie finally spoke up. "Jed, I'm sorry about last night. You were right. You told me not to go out in the canoe by myself, but I really wanted that rice for dinner, and you were gone."

"I shouldn't have gotten mad, Lizzie. You scared me. What would I do without you? I know you are doing better with the canoe, but please don't do that."

Lizzie dropped her head for a couple of steps then reached over for Jed's hand and gave it a squeeze. "Are we okay now? I don't want you mad at me."

Jed nodded, finding himself somewhat sheepish all of a sudden. He had trouble speaking for a moment; something was lodged in his throat when he looked into Lizzie's eyes. "Yeah, we're good."

Lizzie's smile was dazzling, and she gave Jed's hand another quick squeeze before dropping it and walking along with him in a comfortable silence.

Sometime later, with the blackberries nearly in sight, Lizzie spoke up again. "Jed, I was thinking last night. You said you found bees. If we can get enough honey and some honeycomb, I think I could get the beeswax out and use it to cover the fruit we pick. I think I could make some preserves. Do you think we could do that?"

Jed thought for a few minutes. "I think we probably could get some honey. The biggest thing is to get at it. It's fairly high up in a tree, and then we have to see if it's good. This isn't going to be honey like you buy in the store. It's wild, and it won't taste the same."

"I don't think that will be a problem. I just don't know how much I'll need to make beeswax. I'd like to try it."

"All right. Let's see about picking blackberries today, and maybe we can do something about the honey tomorrow. For today, we'd better hurry. It looks like a storm is building."

They hurried toward the patch of blackberries Jed found, mindful of the weather. Hopefully, the rain would hold off long enough for them to pick what they needed.

On the far side of the copse of trees between them and the blackberries, the old sow bear waded into the thicket with her nearly grown cub behind her. She had a taste for blackberries and needed to gorge herself to prepare for winter. She settled in to stripping the berries, not minding the brambles.

Jed and Lizzie stepped into the thicket, ready to start picking. The old sow was across the other side of the thicket, busily eating, and paid them no mind. Jed evaluated the situation carefully. Had he been by himself, he would not have been overly concerned, but with Lizzie along he was more cautious. He had his M1 Garand with him, but the last thing he wanted was to have to shoot the bear.

Whispering, he spoke to Lizzie. "I think we will be okay if we stay on this side of the thicket. She isn't paying much attention to us. She's too busy eating. We'll keep an eye on her, on her cub especially, and get what we can while we're here." They quickly started picking berries. Frequently, they would eat a handful as they picked, giving their lips a dark blue tinge to match their fingers. It didn't take long to fill the smaller buckets, and then pour them into a five-gallon bucket. The old bear paid them no mind, so they continued gathering, looking forward to the treat the berries would provide.

So intent on picking berries and watching the bear, they forgot about the weather. Suddenly, the sky darkened and a strong gust of wind staggered Lizzie. A flash of light and a sharp crack preceded a loud peal of thunder, and it seemed the sky opened up as the rain poured down. Quickly, they gathered their buckets and scurried toward the tree line just behind the blackberry thicket. Jed knew of a rocky overhang not too far away where he had sheltered from the weather on other occasions. He led the way, trying to shield their berries from the rain the best he could.

Once they reached the shelter and ducked under the rocky overhang, they were out of the worst of the storm. "We are better off under here than out under the trees. Lightning won't get to us here. I'll get a fire going in just a few minutes."

Jed slipped out of the shelter and rustled up a couple of handfuls of bark and small twigs and branches from the underside of a fallen tree nearby. He cleared the dried grass and debris from an area and ringed it with small stones. Jed shredded bark and laid on the smallest of twigs before lighting a match and touching it to the shredded bark. Gently, he blew on the glowing bark, bringing a small flame to life, and he soon had a small fire started. Gradually, he put on more small pieces until it was going well enough to put on larger wood. With a hatchet from his belt, he stepped back out into the rain, cut branches from the dead tree, and dragged them under the shelter.

Lizzie, meanwhile, had been caring for the berries, draining the rainwater out of the buckets as best she could to prevent spoilage. She shivered from the chill and was happy to see the fire grow. Soon, she and Jed huddled over the fire, steaming as they warmed and dried. She squeezed as much of the rain out of her hair as she could and then wrapped it in a bun to keep it up. Lizzie was startled as she realized how little it takes for one to be satisfied and happy. Such a difference from three months ago when all she could think about was getting to her own home and being with her daddy. A warm fire out of the storm, and food and fellowship with someone you really liked, was sufficient. Her eyes widened as she glanced over at Jed, recognizing her growing affection toward him. She said nothing but wondered what he was thinking.

CHAPTER 42

C harles Sitton woke up feeling the best he had felt in three months. The time he spent with Sue and Jimmy the night before chased away some of the blues he had been suffering. He smiled, remembering the cheese sauce going down his neck and the confusion that followed. Just because it was not a planned, scripted evening with them dressed up and out in public gave it a much more relaxed, at-home feel. He knew he had developed feelings for Sue, and he thought she had for him as well, although he had not asked. On the one hand, he was excited by what he felt, but on the other, there was a reticence to accept the feelings for what they were, out of memory of his wife.

Despair over his missing daughter also created mixed feelings bouncing between being happy with Sue and Jimmy and despondent when alone. He wished Elizabeth were there to meet Sue. For over a year, Elizabeth had been after him to date, but he had not met anyone who interested him. Though he knew Elizabeth would hit it off with Sue, he hesitated to make his thoughts and feelings known.

Doris Goodland, Charles's secretary, noticed the change in his attitude as soon as Charles walked in the door at work. She had been his secretary for fifteen years and had been with him through the upheaval of the discovery of his wife's cancer and then the futile struggle to defeat it. The last three years had been difficult for Doris as well. The past three months of turmoil had been particularly hard. She and Charles had a very proper, yet close, relationship, transcending boss-employee. To see Charles with a smile on his face meant a lot. She didn't know the cause of his happiness, but she hoped it would continue.

CHAPTER 43

James Romson's morning was not going well at all. He and his wife had noted the three-month anniversary, but unlike Charles they had had no positive input. Attitudes around their home had become rather strained. A call to Detective Summers had not gone well. She still had no answers; in fact, she had no leads to follow. As she said, it was as if the earth had swallowed the plane. There were no reports of a Beaver matching their description anywhere. FBOs around the entire country, and even into Canada, had been queried, but nothing matched. As she told James, "'I don't know' means I don't know."

James tried hard to work, but he was glad he had placed Tran in charge because his thoughts kept wandering to Jed and Elizabeth. The missing airplane was an inconvenience, but what really mattered was the two kids. He would gladly give up the plane to get the kids back. He blamed himself for not giving Pete the money when he asked for it. He couldn't help feeling it was his fault the kids were missing. Yes, he knew such thinking was pointless and self-defeating, but the thought remained in his head.

CHAPTER 44

An hour passed before the thunderstorm settled down to a steady drizzle. Jed and Lizzie decided they would run for it and get back to the cabin to care for the berries.

As soon as they arrived at the lodge, Jed stripped his rifle down and cleaned it so it would not rust, while Lizzie spread the blackberries on the kitchen table to dry. Between the two of them, they ate quite a few, but over two gallons still remained for Jed to dry. He couldn't set them out for drying, though, until the rain stopped.

The storage area was a wreck, but Jed rummaged about until he found the bee smoker and two bee bonnets. If the rain stopped soon, there was a chance they could rob the hive in the afternoon, since he did not want to pick wet berries.

Lizzie busied herself preparing lunch, trying unsuccessfully to keep her mind from dwelling on Jed. It was funny how she had known him all her life, had been in the same classes from kindergarten all the way through her senior year, but had never thought of him other than as a casual friend. She found herself wanting to do something extra special.

After taking a quick look at their greatly diminished supplies, she decided there was just enough flour, sugar, and other ingredients to make a cobbler. She would use some of the blackberries and surprise him. The supplies were saved for something special, and this seemed special enough. Looking outside, she decided Jed was busy and wouldn't be in for a while. Hurrying to save the surprise, she gathered the ingredients and mixed them together. After putting the cobbler in the oven, Lizzie went into her room to brush her hair and make herself look as nice as she could.

Jed walked into the lodge with his hands full of bee bonnets and the smoker. The sky had started to lighten, and it seemed as if the rain was tapering off. The idea of fresh honey was appealing. He sniffed, smelling the aroma of something delicious.

"Hey, Lizzie, what's cookin'?"

Lizzie walked from her room with heart fluttering. She had her hair brushed out and down, instead of tied up in a loose bun like she had been wearing it. Her hair had grown long in the last three months and now reached well below her shoulder blades. She noticed it always caught Jed's eye when she wore it down, although he never said anything. She gathered her hair in her hands and draped it casually over her shoulder for him to notice.

"Oh, it's nothing much. I just made a cobbler."

Jed's mouth watered. Due to their diminished supplies, their diet had been bland lately. Their diet was healthy, but there had been very few sweets or baked goods.

"It smells wonderful!"

Lizzie felt his eyes on her as she walked past him to go to the oven, but he said nothing else.

Jed ate his cobbler slowly, savoring the sweetness of each bite, rolling each morsel around on his tongue. "What's the special occasion? It's not your birthday or something, is it?"

"Oh, no. It's nothing like that. I just thought you deserved something special." Lizzie felt like she had fireworks going off inside as she looked into Jed's eyes. "You'd better enjoy it, because there is no more sugar."

"Oh, don't worry. I am!" With that, he picked up his saucer and licked the remaining juices from the surface, bringing a giggle of delight from Lizzie.

After polishing the saucer with his tongue, Jed asked if Lizzie would go with him to rob the beehive. The hive was higher in the tree than he could reach from the ground, and he wanted help steadying the ladder. The hive wasn't terribly high, but he didn't want to worry about the ladder moving while he was working with bees. Regretfully, Lizzie gathered her hair and wrapped it into a bun, seeing Jed watch out of the corner of her eye. She wondered if he felt for her what she felt for him.

Jed took coals from the stove for the smoker, then, with Lizzie carrying the bee equipment, walked outside and picked up the short ladder needed to climb the tree. He had difficulty carrying the ladder with his rifle slung over his back while also carrying the smoker. The smoker burned his leg every time he bumped it. Lizzie, on the other hand, had her hands full of the bee bonnets, gloves, and a large bucket. Fortunately, they only had to walk about half a mile to the bee tree.

"Look up there, just below the fork in the tree. See the shiny spot by that little hole? Watch. You'll see bees going in and out," Jed whispered.

Lizzie saw several bees coming and going in just a few minutes' time. It was easy to see why the bark was shiny around the hole. Bees landed on the bark and walked into the hole while others crawled out and launched themselves into the air. Thousands of bees had worn the bark smooth. "It's an old hive," Jed whispered. He had no idea why he whispered, like he didn't want the bees to hear him or something. "This tree is probably loaded."

Jed leaned the ladder on a branch to the side and a little lower than the bee hole and settled the base carefully in the dirt before he put on long gloves. He had Lizzie tie a string around the tops of the gloves so there was no gap the bees could access and tied other strings around the bottoms of his pants legs. He helped Lizzie do the same, and then both donned bee bonnets and settled them carefully over their heads. After pumping the bellows on the smoker a few times, he was satisfied with the stream of smoke emanating from the contraption.

"I'll climb up and smoke them well. Hold the ladder steady, and be ready for me to hand the smoker back down to you."

Lizzie nodded and stepped under the ladder where she could grasp it firmly.

Jed carefully climbed the ladder, burning himself once when the smoker brushed against his leg. He placed the nozzle of the smoker into the entry hole and pumped the bellows several times, injecting smoke deep into the hive. Reaching down, he handed the smoker to Lizzie, saying, "Be careful where you set that. It's hot!"

With a hatchet he took from his belt, Jed chopped the hole larger, enough to see inside the tree and to dip out honey. Lizzie handed him the bucket and a long-handled ladle with which he began dipping.

"I knew it. This whole tree is full!"

Jed worked rapidly to fill the bucket before the bees came out of their stupor.

"I doubt we will be able to get any more honey from this hive," Jed remarked as he carried the five-gallon bucket, nearly full of honey, back to the lodge. "The bees will more than likely find another place and will move the honey. I tried to disturb the hive as little as possible, but since I had to enlarge the opening, I doubt they will stay. We'll watch and see." He would come back in a day or so and check. If the bees moved, as he suspected they would, he would recover the ladder, since it was more than he could carry with the bucket of honey. Lizzie carried the smoker and the bee bonnets, and her mouth watered. The honey smelled sweet, and she didn't think it smelled very wild. Her mind raced with ideas of what she could make with it.

CHAPTER 45

For three weeks, Jed and Lizzie worked from "can see to can't see" to pick and store as many blackberries and blueberries as they possibly could. Jed thought it probable they would over-winter in the lodge, and he was doing all he could to prepare. If they were rescued before winter, it would be wonderful, but if not they had to be prepared. He noted the shorter evenings with misgiving, knowing the long, cold winter nights were pressing closer and closer.

Although they had been in close proximity to the old she-bear, and she had woofed threateningly at them on a couple of occasions, they had no problems with her. She was more concerned with preparing herself for winter than she was with them. They were cautious around her and especially the nearly-grown cub, careful to give them plenty of space and remain far enough away to not present a threat.

Smoking and drying fruit had become a full-time job, and Jed left it to Lizzie to accomplish. He was concerned about the lack of firewood he had stockpiled for winter. All of the deadfall wood close to the lodge had been gathered already, so Jed had to go farther, which made a lot of hard work carrying wood back to the lodge.

There was a chainsaw in the storage shed and a fair supply of gas and oil for the saw, but there was not a power wood splitter available, so he did a lot of work with a sledge and wedges. Lizzie noted, with a little thrill, the added muscle he developed by swinging the sledge.

Jed had contrived a travois of sorts for dragging loads, but it was still slow, hard, hot work. The rapidly changing leaves added urgency to their work. Frost on the roof in the morning made Jed's heart lurch.

When Lizzie finished a gallon of preserves from each of the blueberries and blackberries, and dried and smoked the remainder, she started gathering hazelnuts. Deer and squirrels were devouring them, so she had to hustle to get what they needed.

Jed carried the hazelnuts to the lodge for her and spread them to dry on the extra bunks. When the husks dried well and the nuts were loosened in the husks, they took turns treading on them in the bottom of a barrel, separating the nuts from the husks.

"When we get back home, I'll never complain how hard it is to do things again!" exclaimed Lizzie. "I never realized how much work went into doing things in the old days. My grandmother used to try to tell me how differently we had it than they did, and she didn't even have to do all of this."

"I know. It's hard to believe people lived like this just a hundred years ago. We have it so easy!"

CHAPTER 46

Detective Summers tried hard not to get her hopes up. A report filtered through the grapevine of a float plane landing and taking off from desolate lakes in Minnesota at night. All indications from informants pointed to drug running, with a truck meeting the plane during the night. As of yet, the plane had not been identified, but area farmers' descriptions matched the missing Beaver, down to the colors and markings.

Discreet inquiries of Jed's friends and classmates had not brought up any hints of drug involvement nor of any sort of illegal activity on Jed's part, but he would not be the first to hide something of the sort. Most criminals talked their way into jail, or someone they knew did it for them. Sooner or later, it came out if those in law enforcement were listening.

Chief Washington permitted her to travel to Minnesota, even though it was out-of-state and out of her jurisdiction. She was to liaise with the local authorities and possibly assist with their surveillance. Nothing about her travel and participation fitted normal protocol, but

Chief Washington was as anxious to find the missing teenagers as was Detective Summers. He still met James Romson at least twice a week at Kiwanis and at other civic functions, besides speaking on the phone at least once a week. He hated to look James in the eye and shake his head. Something had to show up sooner or later.

Detective Summers looked at her watch for the fifth time in as many minutes. Over four hours of driving remained, and driving was not something she enjoyed. She wanted to be there, not drive there. She was tempted to turn on her lights and go faster. And she could probably get away with it. After all, police officers generally gave other officers a little leeway, and with the lights flashing it would look official. But she knew it wasn't right, and with her cruise control on she seemed to creep along with everyone else. Sometimes, ethics and integrity just got in the way.

CHAPTER 47

James and Mary walked into Pastor Shepherd's office and sat down. They had come to the conclusion they needed help. As often happens following a tragedy in a family, their relationship had become strained, with tension building to the point they had begun taking their frustrations out on each other. James struggled with sleeplessness as the loss of Jed brought back painful memories of the friends he had lost in Vietnam. Mary recognized James's sense of loss but felt he didn't care about her own loss of her son. Both knew their feelings were irrational but didn't know how to handle matters.

Pastor Shepherd spoke with them about the stages of grief and in particular how theirs was so much different than in the case of death. They had no closure, and the constant reminders of Jed's absence were compounded by the hope he might be found alive. Pastor Shepherd's experience as a chaplain in the Army and extensive dealings with PTSD were crucial for dealing with James. After talking and praying together, James and Mary walked from his office holding hands, determined to weather the storm together. It would not be easy—losing a son never is—but they, with God's help, were determined to make it.

CHAPTER 48

Charles Sitton threaded a worm on a hook for Jimmy. He had taken a liking to the boy and had become somewhat of a father figure in the last couple of months. Charles always wanted a son, but after Elizabeth was born he and Collette were unable to have any other children. Jimmy did a lot to fill the void in his life, at least during the day. Nighttime was still a struggle, and as much as he hated them, he found he still needed the sleeping pills at night.

Jimmy saw his bobber bounce and jerked the line. When he got it in, of course, there was nothing on it.

"You've gotta be a little more patient there, young'un. Wait till he takes it under, then you just give it a little twitch. You start to reel it in if it stays underwater."

"I know. I just got excited and forgot."

"That's all right. It's how you learn."

Charles untangled some of the moss and weeds from the hook and bobber. Jimmy still had to learn how to get the line out of the water without going through the weeds.

"Looks like you still have enough worm. Give it another try."

Jimmy cast the line back out but got it tangled in the weeds again.

Charles chuckled. "Bring it back in and give it another try. Remember this time to let the button go when the rod is halfway there."

Charles shook his head in frustration. To think such a good kid as Jimmy could be fourteen years old and not have had someone to teach him. He didn't know what to think about someone like Jimmy's father, who had messed things up so badly. Jimmy needed Charles as much as Charles needed someone like Jimmy.

Next week they were going to a firing range so Charles could teach Jimmy how to properly shoot and care for a weapon. He thought they would start out with a .22 and work their way up. One thing was for sure, Jimmy was not a sissy.

CHAPTER 49

eechnuts began to fall, along with the leaves. Though the beechnut was small and somewhat difficult to process, it was one of the most important food sources in the wild. Jed knew beechnuts had a high caloric value, and, most importantly to him and Lizzie, they had a high fat content. Getting enough fat in their diet was difficult. Turkeys, deer, and bears would be feasting on the nuts.

Jed went to gather beechnuts with Lizzie because of the bears. The old sow bear seemed to have grown accustomed to their presence and had never threatened, but Jed was aware the black bear was more likely to attack a human than even the feared grizzly bear.

Lizzie looked puzzled when Jed walked out of the lodge before sunup with two sheets in his arms. He put them into the baskets she held and then took the baskets from her.

"What are those for?"

He grinned at her. "Magic sheets! They gather beechnuts."

"What are you talking about? How can you pick up nuts with sheets?"

"Magic," is all he would say.

He led the way toward a group of beech trees. The light grew brighter as they walked, with the sun rising just before they arrived at the beech grove. Two deer, a doe and a fawn, bolted from the trees as they approached.

"That's sign enough of beechnuts. The deer love them."

Jed set the baskets next to one of the tree trunks and started rustling in the leaves with his foot. When he found one of the odd-shaped spinney husks containing the nuts, or masts, as they are sometimes called, he picked it up and showed it to Lizzie.

"Here's why we have the magic sheets, Lizzie. See how small this is?"

The three-sectioned hull was only slightly more than an inch long, and not quite as wide.

"These get lost in the leaves, and trying to find enough to bother with would take days. We don't have enough time for that."

Jed broke open the husk and removed the three small nuts, one from each pod. The nuts were only a little over half an inch long, and were triangular in shape. Each nut had a hull surrounding it.

"These things are tiny, and it takes some work to get at them, but we are going to need their fat for the winter. Deer, birds, other animals—bears in particular—use these to fatten for the cold."

He slit the side of the hull with his thumbnail and removed the nut. Lizzie took it when he held it out to her and gingerly nibbled at the nut, hoping it tasted good.

"This is not bad. A little bit strong, but I think I like it."

"Good. Let's pick what nuts we can reach on the tree first—it's a lot easier than picking them up off the ground—then we will use the magic sheets."

"You keep calling them that. How do they work?"

"Let's pick what we can first, and then I'll show you."

With a basket each, they started working their way around the first tree, plucking the nuts from the tree. They picked steadily, working their way around all the trees in a short amount of time. Lizzie enjoyed the chance to spend the time out-of-doors with Jed and to participate in collecting some of the food supplies instead of being cooped up in the lodge. She didn't mind the housekeeping, but being out with Jed was a real treat.

When all they could reach had been picked, Jed set his basket down by the tree trunk and walked to the tree where he had left the "magic" sheets. Grabbing the sheets, he carried them back to Lizzie. He spread one of the sheets on the ground and said, "Magic Sheet, do your magic!" Lizzie looked at him strangely, like he had flipped.

"Young lady, every magician needs a beautiful assistant. Will you be mine?"

Jed's comment gathered a giggle and a faint blush from Lizzie. Jed had never commented on whether he thought she was pretty or not. She knew he was just joking but hoped there was really something behind his comment.

"I should be most honored, most noble magician," she said with a curtsy.

"Really, I forgot to bring along a rake, so this is going to be a little more difficult. We'll bring one next time. What we need to do is gather all the leaves and stuff from the ground onto the sheet." Jed started scraping the leaves with his feet, kicking them toward the waiting cloth. "Try to get as much of the stuff as you can. I know we will miss some, but I think it would be better to get what we can while we are here rather than wait until next time." Together they swept up a large pile of leaves.

"Now grasp your corners of the sheet and pick it up." Jed started shaking the sheet up and down gently, moving the corners in toward each other and then spreading them back out, causing the sheet to sag in the center, and then rise back up. Some of the top leaves flew off, but he told Lizzie not to worry about them. After a few minutes they laid the sheet on the ground, and Jed carefully swept the leaves from the top of the pile, exposing the beechnuts that had settled to the bottom.

"See how great the magic sheet is?" laughed Jed. Lizzie just shook her head and moved her basket by the sheet. "Now, put your end of the sheet into the basket." Jed lifted his end of the sheet and poured a good portion of the gathered beechnuts into the container.

CHAPTER 50

T he old she-bear was cranky. A long thorn was stuck in her foot between two pads and was infected. Because of its location between the pads, she was not able to get it out either with her teeth or by licking it.

Her nearly-grown cub was frisky in the chilly morning air and tried to play with her when he awoke. She swatted him hard enough to send him rolling, when she would normally have just brushed him aside or perhaps woofed at him in warning.

The blueberries were now gone, but the old bear knew the beechnuts were dropping. She limped through the underbrush toward the largest copse of beech trees in her territory. Her cub, chastened, followed behind but wandered off a little ways, following the fragrance of honey. The bee tree Jed and Lizzie robbed was empty, as Jed had thought it would be, but the cub climbed the trunk to the opening. He snuffed loudly and reached his long tongue into the hole to lick at the remnants stuck to the sides of the hollow tree. Finally, frustrated at his inability to reach any more honey, he backed down the tree trunk and wandered along the path until he found his mother's scent.

Jed and Lizzie were on their way back to the cabin, their baskets full. The "magic sheets" had been stashed in the crotch of a tree where they wouldn't blow away. Jed didn't want to carry them with the full baskets of nuts and then bring them back. Because they had taken the time to pick the low-hanging beechnuts, they had worked their way to the far side of the grove. Lizzie walked on while he stashed the sheets and was about a hundred yards ahead. The bear sow had crossed her path a few minutes before and was downwind of Lizzie. The bear stood on her hind legs, sniffing the breeze, troubled by human presence. Normally, she would not have been concerned, but she was cranky, and the smell irritated her. Bears have good eyesight, but since bushes were in the way, Lizzie couldn't be seen. She settled back down onto her sore foot and resumed rummaging in the leaves for nuts.

The cub, however, was upwind and didn't smell Lizzie ahead of him. It is hard to say who was more startled when the cub rounded a clump of brush and nearly ran into Lizzie. She screamed and dropped her basket as the cub gave a startled woof and ran away.

The old sow bear, already on edge, heard her cub's cry and charged. Since a black bear can run as fast as thirty-five miles an hour for a short distance, Lizzie had no chance of outrunning her. They also climb trees, so she knew climbing was not an option. She dropped to the ground and lay there motionless and tried hard not to cry or show any signs of life but prayed desperately under her breath.

CHAPTER 51

Detective Summers lay in deep weeds inside a tree line near the Minnesota lake she had come to investigate. Sheriff Jake Larson had been more than willing to have her come along on this surveillance stakeout.

"TV never shows this side of law enforcement does it, Jake?"

The sheriff snorted and shook his head.

Two weeks before, on the promise of a lighter sentence, an informant told one of the deputies a drug shipment was due at this lake. Tonight was the last of the possible nights the informant said the plane might come. The sheriff and ten of his men, plus Detective Summers, had hidden in the weeds each night for the last six nights, fruitlessly. Expecting a lookout to be posted, they infiltrated the area, walking over two miles through some rough, brushy areas. It was now two o'clock in the morning, and they had been in position since before nine the previous evening. Under normal circumstances, the sheriff would have posted a single officer to observe and then would have made plans to make the raid based on his surveillance. But due to the infrequent and sporadic visits by the plane, he didn't feel he could waste the opportunity to make the arrests now.

A few minutes after two in the morning, the sound of a small vehicle could be heard driving down the dirt access road leading to the field a hundred yards beyond the lake and their position. Everyone perked up but remained in place. Each person on the surveillance team heard the sheriff's quiet "Hold in place; maintain silence! Everybody check in" through their digital radio earpieces.

Each of the ten deputies clicked his microphone button once in turn, showing all were awake and alert.

It was a full five minutes before a Toyota Land Cruiser eased into the clearing, its way lighted by headlights heavily taped over, leaving only a small slit for light. The driver drove past the lake to the field before turning around and returning to the lake and parking the SUV in a small cleared spot in the underbrush. Sheriff Larson noted the back lights and brake lights were disconnected, so no light was visible from the rear either.

Sheriff Larson broke his own rule by leaning over to Detective Summers and whispering, "Stupid fool. If he had driven back here with his lights on, he would have had deniability for being here. They outsmart themselves most of the time." He whispered into his microphone, "Hold in place."

The driver turned off his engine and sat with his windows rolled down for a few minutes, listening to the night. When he heard nothing suspicious, he got out of the truck and looked carefully around. Detective Summers could clearly hear him speak into a walkie-talkie. "In position. Starting a walk around now. Stand by."

Each of the deputies could see the driver through his night vision goggles, or NVGs, as the driver walked along the brush line, looking into the brush to see if anyone was there. Fortunately, they were all far enough away and had camouflaged themselves. In the dark, they were invisible to him unless they moved. The eye picks up movement readily, but motionless they were secure. Fortunately, the lookout did not have infrared goggles or NVGs. When he was halfway around the lake, one of the deputies heard the lookout's walkie-talkie beep, and the message "What's the word? The plane is half an hour out."

"I need about fifteen minutes to finish going around the lake unless you want me to quit checking."

"No! You have to check. You haven't done anything illegal, so if you are stopped, there isn't anything they can do to you. Always follow procedure!"

"Okay. Tell the pilot to delay a little so I can finish and get the lights set up. I need about forty minutes."

"K. Hurry all you can. We can't have him circling and getting people suspicious."

When certain the lookout was well out of hearing, the deputy responsible for surveilling the far side of the lake whispered into his radio what he heard. Everyone perked up, excited, but remained in position.

The lookout moved at a trot around the rest of the tree line, looking carefully but hurrying. He picked up the walkie-talkie. "All clear. Send the truck. Stand by on the plane." From his car, he pulled a surveyor's tripod and ran to set it up near the water's edge. He installed a small strobe light on the top and turned it on.

"Light's lit," he said on the radio. "Send him in."

A rental truck with all lights extinguished crept down the lane until it reached the SUV. The driver jumped out of the truck, walked to ten feet from the water, and started screwing a guy wire anchor post into the ground. When he was done, he carefully stepped off twenty paces and screwed another in place.

Detective Summers could hear an airplane approaching. From where she lay in the brush, she couldn't see it, tempting as it was to step to the edge of the brush and look. The driver of the rental truck eased the truck back toward the water, guided by one of two men who had ridden in the truck.

CHAPTER 52

James Romson sat in his office with papers spread across his desk but without the focus he needed to address the issues. He picked up his phone and dialed Chief Washington's private line.

"Jeff, James here. I've been unable to reach Detective Summers for several days now. Do you know what's going on? Any progress?"

As much as he wanted to, Chief Washington could not say where Detective Summers was, nor could he say what she was doing. He thought quickly. "Hi, James. Detective Summers is out of town on an investigation for me. I talked with her last evening, and she has nothing to report." He knew what he said, while true, was not totally honest, but it was the best he could do. "I'm really sorry, James. You know that. I can assure you we are doing all we possibly can do. 'I don't know' still means I don't know."

"Yeah, I know. I'm sorry to keep bothering you." Discouragement was evident in James's voice.

"Hang in there, James. We're trying."

"I know. I appreciate you letting me call you and bug you. You don't have to do that, I know. Mary and I appreciate it." He slowly hung the handset on the receiver and walked through the door to Tran's office.

James laid a stack of papers on Tran's desk. "I'm sorry, my friend, but I need you to take care of these projects for me. I can't keep my mind on work today. I think I'll go home."

Tran rose from his desk chair and walked around the desk. "James, my friend, this will all work out." Uncharacteristically, the smaller man put an arm around his boss and friend and gave him a quick hug. "Set your mind at rest. We have the office covered, and I have time to take care of the paperwork. Go home and take Mary out, do something fun, and take your mind off of things."

"I think I've forgotten how to do something fun."

"James, can worrying change things? Did we ask God to take care of matters? If we put things in God's hands, don't try to take them back out and hold them in your hands. You can't fix things. Go find Mary and spend some happy time with her. She needs it as badly as you do."

James straightened his bowed head. "Thank you, my friend. That's good advice. But it's hard for me to do. I always want to be in control of things. I guess if I ask God to do it, He doesn't need me getting in His way, does He?"

James gave him a tired smile, walked out of the office, and headed home to find Mary.

CHAPTER 53

J ed heard Lizzie scream and the cub bawl and dropped his baskets. He ran toward her, unleashing the rifle from his back as he ran. He saw the bear cub running away and Lizzie curled on the ground, but he could not see the old bear. Jed could hear crashing in the leaves and brush, so he knew he had little time. There was only a small area open enough for a shot, and that would have to be a very quick one if he was going to have a chance. Jed dropped to a knee, wrapped the sling around his arm, and brought the rifle to his shoulder. He looked for a sight picture in the first open spot he would have. His odds of killing the bear with one shot were miniscule at best, and he breathed a quick prayer just as the old sow bear crashed through the last bush into the open space.

Jed knew a heart or a lung shot was his best chance. He aimed directly behind the shoulder and fired. He followed the bear with the rifle but didn't have opportunity for another shot due to brush. But he didn't need one. His shot was deflected by a twig just enough that, rather than hitting the bear in the heart or lungs, it severed the spinal cord, paralyzing the bear. Her forward momentum was enough that her nose nearly hit the bottom of Lizzie's shoe when the bear came to rest, snapping her jaws, but unable to move her legs. Jed's prayer was answered!

Jed ran forward, carrying his rifle at ready, anxious to protect the one he loved. The one he loved? The thought hit his mind, staggering him, and he almost fell.

Yes, the one he loved. He had not noticed his feelings before now, having become accustomed to her presence, but taking her for granted. There had been a growing attachment and dependence on Lizzie for some time now. Whenever he was out and away from the lodge, he looked forward to getting back to the cabin and showing Lizzie what he had achieved. Wonder filled his mind as he knelt down next to the quivering and crying Lizzie. Gently, he lifted her from the ground and cradled her.

"It's okay. I got her. She can't hurt you."

"I know. I knew you would. You wouldn't let anything hurt me. I'm just being a baby."

"Honey, you are anything but a baby! I would have been frightened out of my mind if it was me."

"What did you call me?" Lizzie leaned her head back so she could look Jed in the eyes. "Did you just call me honey?"

"I don't know. Did I?"

Lizzie looked up into Jed's eyes and a wan smile crossed her tear-streaked face. "Yes, you did. Did you mean it?"

Jed nodded. "Um-hmm. Lizzie, I love you. I just realized how lost I would be without you!" Jed's eyes started tearing now. "I'm kind of dense. It took something like this to make me realize I really do love you! Do you think you could possibly love me, too?"

Lizzie hugged Jed tightly. "Oh, Jed! I've been in love with you for quite a while now! I knew you wouldn't let anything happen to me! I know you love me, too, but it just took you a while to figure it out. Guys are always slow about things like that," she teased. Jed knew she was going to be all right if she could joke, even as she quivered from fear, but her faith in him was frightening. What if he failed her? Suddenly, the responsibility placed on him struck home.

Jed's voice was shaky, but he quipped back, "Well, I have wanted a bear rug for the lodge. If I would have known how easy it would be, I would have used you for bait a long time ago!" He leaned back quickly to avoid the swat on the arm she gave him but didn't succeed.

They huddled together on the ground for quite some time before the shakes quit and they could continue back to the cabin.

CHAPTER 54

The sound of an aircraft engine grew louder. The lookout was clear of the lake, and the men from the truck looked to the west. A float plane with all lights extinguished was approaching, but only visible as a shadow, obliterating the stars. At the last minute, a landing light flared on as the plane was on a straight-in approach to the lake. The pilot chopped power and splashed down in the water, quickly extinguishing the landing light as he increased power to taxi the plane to shore, guided by two lighted wands held by the lookout. The pilot nosed the plane to the bank and shut down the engine.

While the men on shore pulled the back of the plane to the shore and secured the float, front and back, to the two anchor posts, the pilot jumped down from the plane and walked to the truck.

Detective Summers was excited. The plane was a Beaver, and its color and markings matched the description of the Romson Industries aircraft. The N-number, close but different, could have been changed. Nervous, she looked over at the sheriff, waiting for him to make a move, but he just lay there watching intently. He lifted a hand slightly, signifying to wait. They watched, silent, as the cargo door of the plane was opened and the truck backed almost to water's edge. The truck's loading ramp was extended, but instead of putting it on the ground, the end was extended into the hold of the aircraft. Two men pulled bales of marijuana from the plane and carried them across the ramp into the truck. A third man jumped into the back of the truck and re-emerged a moment later, pulling a hose with which he started refueling the airplane.

The pilot nearly ruined the whole setup. He walked into the woods, seeking to relieve himself, and almost stepped on the sheriff. Startled, with a shout he started to run back to the plane, but Sheriff Larson reached out and tripped him.

"Take them down now!" he said into his radio.

Detective Summers jumped on the pilot's back, pinning him to the ground with a knee on the back of his neck, and yelled, "You are under arrest. Let me see your hands."

Each of the deputies jumped up and shined powerful, handheld spotlights on the smugglers. Sheriff Larson called out on a bullhorn, "You are under arrest. Get on the ground now!"

The deputies converged on the suspects as engines and sirens could be heard and flashing lights could be seen as squad cars raced down the access road to assist.

Only one suspect tried to flee. He ran for the woods but was promptly tackled by a deputy. All of the smugglers were cuffed and gathered at the truck where their rights were read.

Detective Summers walked to the plane. Climbing into the cabin she checked the ID numbers, and her heart sank with disappointment. She knew the odds of it being the right plane were slim, but she had still hoped. Climbing out of the cockpit onto the float, she looked at the fuel hose in the tank and then followed the hose back inside the truck, where she saw two fifty-five-gallon drums of avgas and an electric pump. So that's how they did it!

By the time the prisoners were processed and the crime scene secured, the sun was up and the day well begun. Detective Summers shook hands with Sheriff Larson and thanked him for allowing her to participate. She had not found the plane she was looking for, but she had some answers to other questions. Though tired, she knew she was way too keyed up to sleep. She would try to get some miles behind her before getting a room. She also needed to call and touch base with the chief. She would wait, though, until she returned home to talk with the Romsons and Charles Sitton.

CHAPTER 55

Jimmy was proud of the fish he carried into the house. He had not caught anything large, but for his first time he had not done badly. He had two bass between two and three pounds each and two bluegill about the size of Charles's hand, and Charles assured him they were the perfect size for eating. Charles had caught half a dozen bluegill and another small bass. For him, it wasn't much of a catch, but then they had been fishing from the bank with worms, and he had been focused on teaching Jimmy. Charles realized he had had more fun fishing from the bank and teaching than he usually did fishing for larger fish from a boat. Seeing Jimmy's excitement whenever he got a nibble was contagious.

After showing off Jimmy's catch to Sue, Charles took Jimmy into the backyard to teach him how to clean fish. Though not the most enjoyable task, Jimmy insisted he be allowed to do it all. Charles carefully supervised and voiced his approval when Jimmy was done. Charles's heart ached from not having Elizabeth there with them, but the pride on Jimmy's face was payment in full for the day.

Charles commandeered the kitchen when the fish were cleaned. Sue had a potato salad ready and some baked beans in a crock-pot. Charles mixed a coating for the fish with egg and corn meal and fried the fish in two skillets. Jimmy stayed close by, watching intently as the fish cooked. Sue slipped an arm around Charles's waist and gave him a little squeeze.

"Thank you," she whispered in his ear. "I haven't seen Jimmy so interested in life in a long, long time."

"Hey, no problem! He's a good kid, and I had as much fun as he did. I haven't fished with a worm and a bobber in a long time, and I enjoyed myself. He's kind of filling in for Elizabeth, and I sort of think his mother is special, too."

Sue blushed as she gave him another little squeeze. "I'd better be getting the table set." She hurried into the dining room, wiping her eye when she didn't think Charles would see her. The more she was around him, the more she wanted to be with him. She thought Charles was pretty special, too.

When the fish were done, Charles carefully separated the first fish Jimmy had caught, one of the small bass, and placed it on Jimmy's plate.

"A man should always eat his own first catch. You will catch a lot of fish in your life, but there is only one first fish. Eat it in good health and enjoy."

Jimmy grinned broadly. "Thanks, Mr. Charles. Thanks for taking me! I really had fun."

"Mr. Charles?" Sue asked.

"I got tired of being called Mr. Sitton, but he said you wouldn't let him call an adult by his name, so we settled on Mr. Charles. I hope you don't mind."

"I guess it's okay. I want to be sure he is respectful."

"Oh, don't worry! He is very respectful, but I know how to handle a young lad if he isn't. I'll never have to worry about Jimmy. You've done well with him." He reached over and tousled Jimmy's hair and said, "Right, Jim?"

"Yes, sir!"

"Yes, sir?" Sue looked at her son quizzically.

Charles grinned. "He asked about the Marine Corps and how he could become a Marine. I told him some things and stressed the importance of proper respect. I was just a grunt, not an officer, so I didn't rate 'sir' in the Corps, but he thought it would be appropriate for me. I can't argue with his thinking."

Sue leaned over and gave Jimmy a hug. "I think I like it. It seems my son is growing up all of a sudden."

CHAPTER 56

J ed sent Lizzie back to the lodge with a basket of beechnuts while he started field dressing the old bear. He was glad for the meat. The fat would be good for them, but right now was an inopportune time if they were going to collect nuts and acorns for winter. One took what was available, though, and gave thanks. He would have to help Lizzie a lot over the next couple of days if they were going to preserve so much meat.

Jed started planning even as he removed the entrails from the carcass. Finding enough containers for all the meat was going to be challenging, as well as cooking the meat and saving enough grease to smother and preserve it after it cooked. It wasn't as good as freezing meat, but the weather was not yet cold enough to keep the meat from spoiling. He wished he could have waited another month or two so he could count on the weather being cold enough.

Lizzie hurried back down the trail carrying nylon straps. Jed was in process of cutting down a sapling to go with another he had already cut to make a travois. After he trimmed the small branches, Lizzie helped him weave the straps loosely between the poles to create a platform on which to place the bear. Jed laid the travois next to the bear, and with quite some difficulty they were able to roll her onto it.

There was no way to know for certain, but Jed guessed the carcass weighed close to three hundred pounds. Even with the hide still on the carcass and all of the fat, there was a lot of meat they could count on for the winter.

Jed contrived a harness of sorts so he could use his shoulders to bear some of the weight; then, bending to the task, he began to trudge slowly, dragging the bear behind him. He had considered cutting out some of the better cuts of meat and leaving part of the carcass behind, but he decided wasting it would be wrong.

Lizzie picked up one of the other baskets of nuts and started back ahead of him, hoping to be able to get the other basket before some of the animals took advantage of their work. She was able to walk the two miles to the lodge and back again before Jed managed to go a quarter of a mile. He was obviously tired but determined to make it. Jed was grateful for the bottle of water she brought back to him and drank it down greedily while rubbing his shoulders, which were sore from the straps cutting into them.

Lizzie rushed to gather the spilled nuts from where she had dropped her basket, and back to the lodge she trudged. This much walking was more than she was accustomed to, but she was determined to return right away and help Jed with the bear.

Lizzie hurried back as quickly as she could walk, which was noticeably slower than it had been, but a look of determination was on her face. She carried more strapping, with which she hoped to help pull the bear.

Jed fastened the end of the strap to the travois, in front of the webbing on which the bear lay. Then he fashioned a harness of sorts, fitting it over Lizzie's shoulders and around her waist. She had noticed

Jed rubbing his shoulders where the strapping chafed at them, so she had also brought back some padding. Jed divided it between the two of them, and they started the long trek pulling the bear. By the time they reached the halfway point, the sun was setting and it was obvious they would not make it before dark.

Jed directed Lizzie into a glade where he cleared grass and leaves from a large circle while Lizzie gathered small branches. Once Jed was satisfied the ground was bare enough, he laid down some crushed bark and dry grass and built a small teepee of small twigs over the tinder. Striking a match, he lit the tinder and blew gently to get a small fire started. As it caught he added more twigs and then progressively larger pieces. It was not yet cold, but he knew it would be quite chilly before the night was over. He tried to get Lizzie to go on to the lodge, but she insisted—if he stayed out with the bear, she would also. Jed knew he could not leave the bear out alone, or the coyotes and other animals would eat it.

There was jerky in his pocket. He never left the lodge without some. When out in the woods, one never knows if something will happen to prevent a return when one expects to return, so he always made sure to have something to tide him over. He pulled out two pieces and gave one to Lizzie, and together they chewed in silence. Jed could see Lizzie was exhausted, so when she had eaten he cleared another spot three feet from the fire and laid wood for a new fire. He moved the fire over to the new spot and brushed all of the embers away from the first place. After laying some evergreen branches in a small pile over the area, Jed said, "Lizzie, come lie down here where the fire was. The ground is warm and will keep you warm for a while." He noticed she was already starting to shiver. Stress of the day, exhaustion, and the chilly air had caught up to her.

Lizzie laid herself down and felt the warmth of the ground. She smiled up at Jed. "I learn something new from you all the time! I never would have thought of this."

"It's nothing. Just because you're out-of-doors, you don't have to be uncomfortable. It would be nice to have something to cover up with, but we will be okay."

"Where are you going to sleep?"

"I'll lean against the bear. She still has enough heat to keep me warm enough. I don't want to sleep too deeply in case coyotes or something comes."

"Coyotes? We won't be safe?" Lizzie half sat up.

"No, we'll be fine. Coyotes won't usually attack humans unless they are helpless. That's why we have a fire, and I'll sleep lightly. They won't bother us."

Jed walked away from the fire as Lizzie settled down to sleep. He began to break branches off an old deadfall.

CHAPTER 57

James and Mary walked from the theater holding hands. They started the evening with dinner, followed by a romantic comedy James didn't think he would care for but knew Mary would. Mary snuggled her head on his shoulder as they walked toward the car.

"Thanks, James. I needed that. I think I had forgotten how to laugh."

"I know. Tran basically kicked me out of the office and told me to go have some fun. He was right. We can't do anything about the situation but trust God. I know Jed wouldn't want us moping and fussing the way we have been. Besides, I enjoyed the movie, too. Didn't think I would, but it was funny."

Mary slipped her arm around her husband's waist. "I've got an idea. Let's take off—go somewhere for a week or so. Just take our minds off of things we can't change anyway, and get ourselves back together."

"Great idea. You know what? I'd like to go to the lodge for a few days. Going up there is getting away from your problems." He walked with his head bowed, trying very hard not to let his feelings get away from him.

"How about if we go the other way? The Hendricksons just got back from a cruise. Madge was telling me what a great time they had."

"I don't know. You have to book tickets well in advance for those, don't you?"

"Madge told me they just decided to go. The ships usually have unsold cabins pretty cheap." She looked up at him with excitement in her eyes. "What do you think?"

"Okay. See what you can find. I'll call Tran and tell him I'll be out of touch for the next week or two."

CHAPTER 58

D etective Summers awoke with a start.

Her mind had been so full, and she had been so excited by her findings she had not stopped for anything on her drive home until the alarm on her fuel gauge beeped, alerting her it was nearly empty. It was nearing midday, and she had not slept in over thirty hours and not much all week. Pulling off of the interstate, she fueled her car and, with the lack of sleep catching up to her, drove across the street to a small mom-and-pop motel. Out here in the country, there weren't many options, and it looked clean. It was early for check-in, but when she explained her situation, the proprietor was only too happy to give her a room without any additional charge. Going to her room, she turned on the A/C and then called the chief to report her location before lying down across the bed, fully clothed. Her last thought as she faded off to sleep was how foolish she had been to keep driving so long.

A familiar but strange noise was in her ears. Upon awakening more fully, she recognized it as an aircraft engine running up to full RPMs, then fading as the plane rushed down a runway to take off. She groaned as she lifted her head and looked at the clock radio on the bedside table. It was six o'clock already! She had arrived just before two the previous afternoon. She had slept, unstirring, for fifteen hours.

Pushing herself up from the bed took effort as every muscle in her body protested. She had hardly even rolled over. Struggling to her feet, Sarah opened her bag and gathered clothing for the day before stumbling to the shower. As the water cascaded over her head and she tried to stretch some of the kinks out of her muscles with the shower massage head and hot water, the sound that had awakened her returned to her mind and rekindled thoughts from the previous days. Something tugged at her mind, but she couldn't quite put a finger on it, something to do with an airplane. . . .

CHAPTER 59

Charles Sitton awoke to the stillness of an empty home. As he did every morning, the first thing he did was look at Collette's picture on his dresser. The ache in his heart did not go away, but as he looked at the picture he thought of Sue and how much the two women would have liked each other. He felt almost as if Collette was telling him to let go. For the first time, he felt a real peace in his mind about his situation with Sue and bringing her and Jimmy into his life. She could never replace Collette, but she was doing a lot to ease the heartache. Sue and Jimmy were also helping to ease the pain of Elizabeth's disappearance. Sue would not allow him to give up hope of finding Elizabeth and bringing her back, and Jimmy's excitement at learning outdoors activities was contagious.

He picked up the phone with lightness in his heart he had not felt since Collette died. "Hi, Sue. Got a minute?" It was early, but he knew Sue would be up, getting ready for work.

"Always for you," Sue said with a smile.

For the first time since her ex-husband had run off after beating her nearly to death and then kidnapping their son, she felt like trusting another man. Of course, she had a great friendship with Doctor Lambert, but the friendship was professional, not something to bring out her femininity. For the last four months, Charles had done just that. The spark they felt in the hospital had grown into a glowing ember that warmed her as she had not known she needed.

"I've got a great idea. Jimmy has Friday off from school for a teachers' work day, whatever that is. If you think Doctor Lambert could do without you for a day or two, what do you say we take off somewhere for the weekend? I'll get you and Jimmy a suite and myself a room, and we can get away from things for a while."

"Sounds like fun. Where did you have in mind?"

"I'd like to take you to the lodge, but . . . I don't know. Someplace far away from here and everything going on."

"Let me check and see if I can get off. It sounds like fun! Surprise me. I have to run or I'll be late. I'd hate to get the weekend off because I got fired."

Both chuckled as they hung up. She knew Doctor Lambert would give her the time off, romantic that he was.

CHAPTER 60

Jed awoke with a start. He had gone to sleep sitting against the bear and had slept more soundly than he wished. He couldn't believe how tired he was. Something awakened him, but he wasn't sure what. The fire was burned down to just coals, so he stirred it up a bit to get a light flame and then added more wood. He put on smaller sticks to get it blazing sooner and piled some larger, dry branches on top. As the fire flared up he saw eyes glowing at him from the edge of the darkness near Lizzie. Rising to his feet he picked up his rifle, although he was loath to shoot it and frighten Lizzie. Besides, one never shoots at something if he doesn't know for sure what he's shooting.

Another set of eyes, and then a third set showed up.

Judging by the height from the ground, Jed deduced they were coyotes. He knew coyotes normally don't travel in packs, and they normally don't bother humans. But the bear carcass had attracted their attention, and there was a large group surrounding the fire now. They were hungry and were trying to find a way to get to the carcass, but his presence kept them away.

Jed called out softly, "Lizzie. Lizzie, I need you." She stirred but did not awaken. He called to her again. "Hey, Lizzie. I need you to wake up." This time she stirred and then stretched and opened her eyes. "Sorry, but I need a little help. Can you get up?"

"Sure, what's wrong?"

By this time, the fire had blazed up, giving more light. The coyotes shrank back from the light further as they tried to find a way to reach the carcass.

"Don't be afraid, but we have some coyotes trying to get to the bear. I need some help to keep them away. Don't worry. They shouldn't attack you."

"What can I do?"

"Pick up a stick out of the fire, and be ready to swing it at one of them if he comes close enough. Usually it's enough."

About that time, one of the braver, or at least hungrier, coyotes dashed toward the bear but drew back when Jed stepped toward him. The others edged closer, as if to make a concerted rush. Jed yelled and ran toward one group, which promptly drew back, but others crept forward in their place. Lizzie swung her branch at one venturing a little too close and connected with a solid thump. The coyote yelped and leaped back, hair singed, but he didn't go far. The scent of the bear was just too tempting.

"I hate to do it, but I may have to shoot some of them."

Three coyotes edged around the circle and made a dash together when Jed had his attention on the other side. He quickly turned and snapped off a shot, dropping one of the three, but the other two jumped on the carcass and started tearing at the hide. Lizzie swung her stick at the two of them, but they didn't flinch. Jed couldn't risk another shot because Lizzie was in the way, so he stepped toward the bear with his rifle reversed and swung the butt. He connected with one's head with a loud *crack*, and the coyote fell off. But the other, instead of running away, leaped at Lizzie, teeth bared.

Suddenly, there was a deep battle cry bark, and a black shape leapt from the shadows and collided with the coyote. The battle was short and sharp. Jed turned and fired at two coyotes trying to come from behind him, and Lizzie swung at three others. The coyote that had leapt at Lizzie turned tail and ran from the circle, yelping, with the black creature chasing it. When it saw the coyote was leaving, the black creature turned back toward some of the others and drove them away also.

"Tommy!" Jed cried out.

He finally remembered the name of the dog John Johnson had lost. Tommy had been named jokingly after John's dad. "Tommy, come here, boy."

Tentatively, he walked toward the fire, as if deciding he wanted to be with people again. Jed reached into his pocket and pulled out a piece of jerky, which he extended toward the dog. This time, he didn't throw it but held it so the dog would have to come to him if it wanted the treat. Lizzie knelt down in the dirt and spoke softly and gently to him. Gradually, the dog stretched his neck out and snatched the jerky from Jed's hand. He darted back to safety before gulping it down.

Lizzie continued speaking softly to the dog, holding her hand out to him. He crept slowly back toward her and tentatively reached his nose to her hand, sniffing.

"There you go," she whispered. "Come on. We won't hurt you. You look like you could use some loving. Oh, look, Jed. His collar is too tight. No wonder he's so skinny. He's probably had a hard time finding food small enough to swallow."

Jed reached into his pocket and pulled out another piece of jerky. He handed it to Lizzie to feed Tommy. This time Tommy took it from her hand and only retreated a little way to eat. Lizzie got another piece from Jed, held it in her lap, and called the nearly starving dog back to her. It came close enough for Lizzie to stroke the side of its head once as she softly crooned to him. Though Tommy jumped back without the jerky, he didn't go as far, and, with Lizzie's constant soft crooning, he crept forward again. This time he allowed Lizzie to place her hand on the side of his head as she fed him the piece of jerky. "Good dog," she crowed and stroked his head gently yet firmly. "You're a very good and brave dog. We'll fatten you up if you'll let us." Tommy seemed to like the attention and stood trembling but didn't pull away.

Jed slowly stood to his feet and started to step toward Lizzie, but Tommy stepped between them and growled low in his throat in warning. Jed laughed and said, "Looks like you have a dog."

Pulling the last piece of jerky from his pocket, Jed extended it toward the dog but kept it close enough that Tommy would have to come to him to get it. He also extended his other hand to let Tommy sniff his hand. At first all Tommy did was growl, but he didn't snap. Finally, Tommy allowed Jed to pet his head while Jed fed him the jerky.

CHAPTER 61

When Detective Summers stepped from the shower, she had reached no better conclusion regarding what bothered her about the airplane she had heard. As she dressed in casual clothes for the day, she was grateful to have a travel day and not to have to report in to the office. She could dress as she wished, not in uniform for a change. She was proud to wear the uniform, but sometimes it was nice to be able to dress feminine. She took a last critical look in the mirror, still with the airplane puzzle on her mind, before walking out the door. Just because she wasn't in uniform didn't mean her mind wasn't working.

"Good morning!" said the proprietor from behind the counter when Detective Summers walked into the front office. "May I say you look much better than you did when you arrived yesterday? I take it you slept well?"

"I don't think that's much of a compliment if I looked as bad as I felt. I hardly rolled over once in fifteen hours. Had a little catching up to do, I guess. Tell me something. I thought I heard an airplane take off this morning. I didn't know there was an airport around here."

"Oh, I'm so sorry! No, we don't rightly have an airport. What you heard was Dan Hixon. He does a little crop dusting from his pasture, which is right behind the motel. I keep complaining he wakes my customers up in the morning with that old plane of his. Doesn't do much good, though, as you can tell."

"Not a problem. I might want to pick his brain about a case I'm working on. How would I find him?"

The proprietor pulled out a local map and showed her how to get to the entrance to Hixon's farm. She turned in her key and walked into the attached restaurant that, judging by the number of pickups outside, must be the local meeting spot for coffee and breakfast. She knew that was always a good sign.

"Good morning. What can I get for you, hon?" asked a middle-aged waitress as she slid a glass of water and a menu in front of Detective Summers.

"Let's start with a cup of coffee, and let me save you a trip. Just bring me a sausage and cheese omelet."

"Homemade biscuits or toast?"

"Real homemade biscuits or from a mix?"

"Real 'hand squoze,' as my momma would call them."

"I haven't had real biscuits in a long time. We'll go with those."

"Okay. That's easy enough. Be right up with it."

Detective Summers, being a police officer, had chosen a corner booth where she had a good view of all that happened in the restaurant and of the entrances and exits. She saw a man walk in the door who had marks around his eyes as if he had been wearing goggles. Somehow, she had the feeling this was Dan Hixon, and his aircraft was an open cockpit type. When he started for a booth near hers, she stood and asked, "Excuse me, would you by any chance be Dan Hixon?"

"I guess it depends on who's asking," he replied with a grin. "Do I know you?"

"No, I heard your plane take off this morning, and when I saw you walk in with goggle marks around your eyes, I just made an educated guess. I'm Detective Summers, and I've been up in Minnesota on a case. I could use some help. I'll buy your breakfast if you'll let me pick your brain for a few minutes."

"Hey, now. Wait a minute. I haven't done anything wrong!"

"No, from all I know of you, you are a good man. I just need some help on a case I'm working on. When I heard your plane this morning, it got me thinking."

"Good enough. I'll do what I can for you." Dan walked over to Detective Summers's booth and sat down.

The waitress came over with a cup of coffee and a glass of water for him and said, "It's on the way, Dan. I saw you walk in the door."

Detective Summers said, "Put it on my ticket, please." The waitress looked at Dan with surprise on her face but said nothing.

"I guess it's what I get for being single and can't cook. I'm too predictable. I don't even have to look at a menu anymore. They just bring it to me. Anyway, enough about me. What can I do for you?"

"First off, tell me about yourself. About your flying history."

"Easy enough. I started out in the Army flying rotary wing— that's helicopters—for the 7th Cav in Vietnam. That's the 7th Cavalry (Airmobile) if you aren't familiar with them. From helicopters I transitioned into fixed wing and did a lot of 'bird-dogging,' or observation work, in the O-2, which is the same as the Cessna Skymaster, a push-pull twin-engine plane used for observation. Since I left the Army, I did some bush flying, and lately I've been trying with mixed success to make a living crop dusting. I have an old Ag-Cat that I keep together with baling wire and chewing gum."

"Don't let him kid you, hon. Dan, here, has a good plane that is as well-maintained as any around! He knows what he's doing in the air, too," said the waitress as she set their breakfasts in front of them. "I hope you don't mind, but I held yours until his was ready."

"That's fine, thanks." Detective Summers turned back to Dan as she cut into her omelet. "Are you familiar with the De Havilland Beaver, then?"

"Oh, yes! One sweet airplane! Takes a lot more green than I ever saw to buy one of those, though. Army had some, and I was checked out in them. Flew some of the brass around 'in country' a few times if they were going too far for a chopper. Loved flying the bird but hated putting up with the brass."

"Have you done any amphibian time?"

"Sure. I did quite a bit right after I got out of the service. Did some bush work up in Alaska and Canada for a while. Took me a bit to save the cash to buy the old Cat I fly now. Fun work, but you have to know what you are doing, like crop dusting. No time for flaking out up there."

"Um-hmm. When I heard your old radial fire up this morning, I had the feeling you'd be able to help me. If you were, hypothetically, to steal a Beaver set up with floats, and needed to fly beyond your range, how would you arrange to have someone meet you in an out-of-the-way spot with avgas in a truck? Would it be hard to buy avgas and put it in fifty-five-gallon drums without causing suspicion? Or would the people at the tank farm consider it strange?"

"Okay. Back up a little bit first. What is it hauling, marijuana or something?"

"No, that's what the one we found when I went to Minnesota was carrying. It was a similar Beaver, and it was full, so the truck they were loading the marijuana onto had some fifty-five-gallon drums of avgas on board. They were pumping the gas into the plane. The plane I'm concerned with would have had two kids along. High school seniors, a guy and a girl, so little weight."

"Strange. Steal an airplane and take a couple of kids along for the joyride."

"We think they were kidnapped, although there is an outside chance the boy was in on it. It was his father's plane."

"That puts a whole different light on it. It isn't all that difficult to move a stolen plane if you have the right connections, but kidnapping kids is different. I don't see why he would want to bring anyone else from outside in on it. It is too easy for someone to talk too much. Let me think on this for a minute." Dan pulled a pen from his pocket and started doing some figuring on his napkin. "Did this plane have the original radial engine, or was it one of those modified with a turboprop?"

"I believe it had the turboprop."

"Um-hmm." More figuring went onto his napkin. "Okay, with the upgraded engine, he can carry almost twenty-two hundred pounds of cargo, so assuming he's flying it by himself, he would still be good for about eighteen hundred pounds of cargo. He should be able to get at least six hundred miles' range out of the plane. Where do you think he was headed?"

"We really don't know. We based our search on the max range of the plane, which with modifications is good for about seven hundred fifty miles, but came up with nothing. When I saw what the drug runners were doing, I got to thinking. We know he didn't land at any FBO or marina handling avgas."

"Why would he need to meet someone to get gas? Avgas weighs about six pounds to the gallon, so he would have the weight and room for about three hundred gallons, which should give him at least another eleven hundred miles' range, depending on winds, of course."

Detective Summers looked crestfallen. "I can't believe I didn't think of that. All I could think of was meeting someone for fuel. I can't believe how badly I've handled this case!"

"Hey, now. Don't beat yourself up. You didn't know, and nobody expects you to know everything. I'm glad I was able to help."

"May I call on you again if I have any other questions?"

"Certainly." He handed her a business card. "Just leave me a message if I'm not in. I'll get back to you right away. I'd give my . . . well, a lot to get a job flying one of those birds. That was a lot of fun sometimes, and it surely beats loading poisons onto that old Cat of mine."

"I know the owner will be looking for a pilot as soon as he can get another plane. He's been having trouble finding someone with bush experience who also can do corporate flying. He also is a veteran and tries very hard to put veterans in all key positions in his company. Would you like me to pass your name to him?"

Besides, she thought, *he is kind of cute, and I wouldn't mind a chance to get to know him better.*

Dan handed her another card. "Please pass this along to the owner. I would love a chance to interview for that kind of job."

Detective Summers stood and shook Dan's hand. "Thank you so much for your help."

"It was my pleasure. If I get down your way to apply for the job, would it be okay for me to give you a call and maybe take you to dinner?"

She smiled. "I would love that."

CHAPTER 62

It was chilly when Jed awoke as the sun was just peeking above the horizon. He found himself curled up and shivering. He and Lizzie had enjoyed a warm spell for the time of year, but he guessed the temperature was in the upper forties. When Jed looked at Lizzie, he was pleasantly surprised to see Tommy curled up next to her, sharing body heat.

Breakfast was going to be an issue. He didn't want to leave the bear, but having given Tommy all of the jerky, they didn't have anything else with them. Tommy's head popped up and a soft growl came from deep in his throat when Jed stood. Jed spoke to him softly, and Tommy settled down and put his head back on his paws. Walking around helped remove some of the stiffness caused by Jed's uncomfortable sleeping position, and he felt better than he thought he would.

He found the three dead coyotes he shot during the night, but it was Tommy who had really saved them. Coyotes, he knew, normally would not attack like they did, but when in a group all bets were off.

All three coyotes appeared undernourished, so hunger could have brought on the attack.

Black Labradors are generally pretty docile, but the time surviving in the wild had taught Tommy to defend himself. His collar was too tight, and something was going to have to be done about it. But there was no way Tommy would let him do anything, at least not yet. Perhaps Lizzie could.

"Lizzie," he called softly. "Lizzie."

Lizzie stirred, and Tommy lifted his head again, watching Jed carefully, but he didn't growl.

"Lizzie, I need you to wake up."

Lizzie stretched and then shivered from the chill as she awakened. At first she was startled and then pleased to find Tommy curled up against her.

"I think you have a friend. He growled at me when I got up."

Lizzie sat up and reached toward Tommy, who drew back, but then allowed her to pet his head. When she scratched behind his ears, all hesitancy vanished and he laid his head in her lap, rolling his head from side to side to get both ears scratched.

"Do you think you could get his collar off, Lizzie? It's way too tight."

Lizzie tried to slip her fingers under the collar, but it was so snug she could not do so without choking him. "Let me have your knife, and I'll cut it off."

Jed pulled his KA-BAR from its sheath and stepped toward her. Tommy picked up his head and growled. "Tommy, he's okay. Just settle down, now." Tommy quit growling but watched carefully as Jed came closer.

Jed reached out his hand to Tommy to sniff and said, "It's okay, Tommy. It's just me." Once Tommy was settled, Jed was able to pet his head and scratch his ears. Tommy seemed to like attention but for some reason was still cool toward Jed. Jed grasped his KA-BAR by the back of the blade and extended the haft toward Lizzie. "Be very careful. It's razor sharp."

Lizzie took it gingerly and cautiously slipped the blade under the collar. Tommy didn't like it when the collar pulled on his throat, and he started to struggle, but Lizzie was able to calm him. Then, with a quick slice, the collar dropped from his neck. Tommy shook his head in relief, turning to Lizzie and licking her face.

Jed said, "It's not fair! Tommy got the first kiss!" and he laughed. Lizzie was busy wiping dog slobber from her face as she tried to get away.

"I could use some breakfast, but I think we had best get this old bear back to the cabin right away. We have a lot of work before us if we are going to save this meat and the hide."

Lizzie handed him the KA-BAR and got up from the ground. She walked over to Jed and kissed him on the cheek.

"That's because Tommy wouldn't kiss you," she said and giggled.

CHAPTER 63

James and Mary boarded their cruise ship in Miami, bound for Belize. Though their business focused on northern climes and cold weather, they both enjoyed the tropics and especially scuba diving and snorkeling. The barrier reef in Belize was supposed to have some of the best diving in the western hemisphere, with a wide variety of fishes. Mary also wanted to see the Mayan ruins. James didn't care about the ruins. He had seen all the jungles he wanted to see years before in Vietnam, but if it would make Mary happy, he was up for it.

Though Jed was still on their minds, they had determined to make the most of the trip and enjoy themselves. Worrying and thinking about him was not going to bring him home. Jed was in God's hands, and they had to be careful to trust Him.

CHAPTER 64

Sue was radiant in a long semi-formal gown as she walked out her hotel room door to meet Charles in the lobby. Jimmy, on the other hand, was unimpressed with the need to wear a suit to dinner. He didn't see anything wrong with getting a pizza delivered to the room and chilling there. Besides, suits were for church or funerals or stuff, not for going out to dinner.

Charles looked sharp in a new suit he had bought for the occasion. The Men's Shop had gone beyond their normal excellent service to have it tailored to fit him properly and to do it overnight. He was pleased at the sight of Sue when she exited the elevator, and he couldn't suppress a grin at Jimmy's obvious discomfiture when he followed his mother from the car.

"You look gorgeous, my dear. You are going to make all the other men jealous of me tonight! And you, young man, you look like you are about to cloud up and rain. What's wrong?"

"I don't see what we have to get all dressed up for just to eat dinner. Why couldn't we have just gotten a pizza delivered or something?"

Charles laughed and stopped his hand just before it rumpled Jimmy's not-so-carefully combed hair. "This is for your mom tonight, sport. You and I are the thorns to her rose. You need to learn how to treat a lady and make the night special for her. Women like to dress up and look beautiful, and your mother did a good job."

"Stop," Sue said. "You're going to make me blush. Besides, you are doing way too much for us. This weekend must be costing you a fortune."

"It's not so bad. This is fun to do once in a while, and what is the point in having a fortune, not that I do, if you can't enjoy it? Besides, having a beautiful woman such as yourself on my arm is a real treat. Shall we go?"

He extended his arm, and Sue took it. Together, they walked to the door, with Jimmy trailing, sulking, behind. The hotel doorman opened the door and then waved a cab forward.

When their cab stopped in front of the restaurant, Jimmy asked, "What is this place? It looks like a mansion!"

"It used to be one. It is now a private club and has a wonderful restaurant. Just wait until you see the inside."

Charles had a big smile on his face as he stepped from the cab and held out a hand to assist Sue. Jimmy tumbled out behind them. Charles stopped him and said gently, "Lesson one: This is not Burger King or Pizza Hut. You notice you have a suit on? You can't get in the front door of this club without one. Now, the dress and the club require a different sort of manners than one would expect at a fast food joint. I want you to pay close attention to the other gentlemen here and behave yourself as they do. You are a sharp kid. I know you'll pick up on it quickly. Jumping from a cab like you were on a baseball field won't cut it. Got it?"

Jimmy nodded, abashed. "Sorry."

"No need to be sorry. This is your first time at such an establishment. This is how you learn. Just like going fishing, you have to learn how to handle the situation."

Sue gave him a big smile of gratitude. "We don't have many opportunities for him to learn these things. Thank you for being patient with him."

"Hey, no problem. This is how they learn. I was a lot older before I ever learned, and I'm afraid I embarrassed myself royally."

The doorman swept the door open for them, and with a slight bow said, "Good evening, madam and sirs. Enjoy your evening."

Just inside the door, the maître d' greeted them. "Good evening, Staff Sergeant Sitton. It is a pleasure to have you in the house again."

Sue was surprised by Charles's reaction. Normally, one would expect to follow the maître d' to the table selected for you, but when the maître d' put out his hand to shake, Charles grabbed it and pulled him into a tight embrace. Sue saw real emotion in both men's eyes as they hugged.

As Charles disengaged, he turned to Sue and said, "Sue, I want you to meet Little Timmy Wright, one of the guys James and I served with." Sue looked up at all six feet, six inches of "Little Timmy" and saw all two hundred seventy pounds was muscle. "If it wasn't for Little Timmy, I wouldn't be here tonight. He got the Silver Star for pulling James and me back to safety. Don't let his Little Lord Fauntleroy suit fool you. This man is the real deal.

"Timmy, would you believe Sue was the anesthesiologist and chief surgical nurse in Tokyo General when they put me and James back together? We've been living in the same town all these years without knowing it."

Charles's revelation generated a hug between Sue and Timmy and a mutually murmured "thank you" from each of them. "I've got to get you to your table before JC comes out and wants to see what all the commotion is. Besides, you have all the guests staring."

He turned and led the way to the center table where, with a flourish, he seated Sue, and then he turned to a bewildered Jimmy and extended a hand.

"I presume this is your mother, young man?"

Jimmy nodded. "Yes, sir."

"You have excellent taste, young man. Take good care of her for me. If she helped put the staff sergeant together again, she is better than all the king's horses and all the king's men. We didn't expect him or James to make it."

Putting a hand on Sue's shoulder, Timmy whispered, "Thanks, again. It is a real pleasure to have you in the house." Surreptitiously, he wiped one eye as he turned and walked away from the table.

In moments, a server set water goblets before them. "I know you don't drink, sir, but will madam be having a glass of wine?"

"Oh, no thank you. I don't drink either."

"Would madam care for iced tea?"

"Tea would be splendid. Thank you."

"And how about you, young sir?"

Jimmy, overwhelmed by the experience, had been paying attention enough to reply, "Yes, thank you."

"Very good. Dinner will be served in just a few moments." And the server walked away.

"He didn't take your order?"

Charles smiled at Sue. "Timmy already knows what I want. I never order when I come here."

"Why do you call him Timmy? I never saw anyone look less like a Timmy than he."

Charles laughed. "You remember Tiny Tim singing 'Tiptoe Through the Tulips,' back in the sixties?"

"Of course, but what does Tiny Tim have to do with Timmy?"

"Well, when Timmy first reported in to Fox Company, he said, 'Wright, Timothy P., reporting for duty,' but he had laryngitis, and his voice came out squeaky. Biggest man in the outfit, but rather than calling him Tiny Tim, they started calling him Little Timmy, and the name stuck. Nobody but those of us who served with him had better ever call him that, but those of us from Fox Company don't ever call him anything else."

Jimmy looked puzzled. "You don't come here often; how can he know what you want?"

"Two things, Jim." Intentionally he removed the diminutive from Jimmy's name. "First of all, Timmy is the consummate maître d'. He excels at his job and learns what his customers' desires are, without having to ask every time. Then, too, he and JC, who is the chef by the way, and I used to sit by the hour and make up menus and recipes when we pulled guard duty at night.

"JC was a chef when the draft caught him, but what did the Marine Corps do with him? They made him a machine gunner! He used to make deals with the Vietnamese locals for fresh produce and meat and cooked for the outfit. We were more than happy to take some of his duties so he could cook. Lot better than C-rats, let me tell you!"

"C-rats?"

"C-rations is what the Corps called them. We had other names, but C-Rats is the most polite. Pre-cooked and canned meals that would keep you alive, but that was about it. We hated them royally.

"Anyway, the captain came by one night when JC was cooking, and he gave the company cook a rifle and unofficially made JC cook. Best thing for company morale ever!"

It was then the kitchen doors swung open with a flourish and a very tall, very black man in immaculate whites and a high master chef's hat on his head rolled a kitchen cart laden with small dishes into the dining room. He was closely followed by two servers, one of whom carried a tray with three iced teas.

Charles didn't wait for them to arrive at the table to serve. He jumped to his feet and, with emotion showing on his face, stepped into a close embrace with the chef, JC. As the servers placed the small serving dishes and iced teas on the table, Charles led JC around the table to meet Sue.

"Sue, I want you to meet JC, one of the closest and best friends a man could ever have. I told you Timmy received the Silver Star for dragging James and me back to safety; well, it was this man who exposed himself to enemy fire to provide covering fire to allow Timmy to get us. A grenade landed at Timmy's feet, and JC threw himself on top of it. Fortunately, the grenade was a dud, but it might not have been. JC also received the Silver Star. It should have been higher, but the chair warmers back at Eighth and Eye—Marine Corps Headquarters, at Eighth and I Streets in Washington, DC—decided it was only worth a Silver Star."

"Stop it, Charles. If I could, I'd blush!" Both men laughed. Sue stood to her feet and, pulling JC down, kissed him on the cheek. Tears were in her eyes as she said, "I'm in your debt, JC. Thank you for saving this wonderful man."

"Ah, but the circle is not broken, JC," Charles said. "Sue, here, was chief surgical nurse in Tokyo General when they put me and James back together."

JC leaned down and kissed both of her cheeks in return.

"I am truly honored, ma'am. All I did was my job. This guy should have been decorated a number of times, but there were no officers around to see what he did."

"You are my heroes, you and Timmy. Thank you." Carefully, trying not to smear her makeup, Sue blotted at her eyes.

"What am I doing? Your food is getting cold! Please, sit down, sit down. We'll get acquainted over dessert. I have to get back to the kitchen before I get fired." JC winked at Charles, stuck a hand out to the bewildered Jimmy, and said, "I'll meet you officially later, young man. We'll go up to the Company Room." JC cast a quick glance around the room to be certain everyone was properly cared for before sweeping back to the kitchen.

"What I had JC do was recreate some of the dishes he made for us when we were 'in country.' Some may seem a mite strange to you, and if you don't like them, you can give them to me and eat the ones you do like. I like them all. Jim, I want you to be acquainted with these men. You will never have a better opportunity to meet better men, nor better role models."

CHAPTER 65

Detective Summers arrived at the police department late in the evening. It had been a long drive home, and she had been held up once by an accident. There was nothing needing her attention yet tonight, so she parked her unmarked squad car in its spot and moved her gear to her own car.

Dan popped into her mind as she drove out the driveway. For some reason, going home to an empty apartment was very lonely. She had to be sure to call James Romson with Dan's information first thing in the morning.

CHAPTER 66

I t was a long, long, hot day. Jed rubbed his forehead wearily with the back of his hand. After dragging the bear's carcass the last mile, most of it uphill, Jed skinned it carefully, then built a fire in both the cookstove and the fireplace, plus in the fireplace outside. Explaining to Lizzie the need to cook the meat thoroughly to prevent trichinosis, he showed her the pages in the cookbook explaining the preservation process of precooking the meat and covering it in melted grease. The grease prevented contact with air, thus preventing contamination or spoilage. It was not the best way to preserve meat, but it was the best they had available. It would prevent them from getting sick, and the meat would go a long way to provide for them through the winter.

Lizzie wore one of her well-worn T-shirts and a pair of shorts instead of her buckskins, but even so her face was sweat-streaked, and tendrils of hair pulled from her ponytail were hanging around her ears. She had the large cast iron pot hanging from the crane over the fire in the fireplace and was stirring the meat and broth with a long-handled spoon.

Jed looked in the door and thought she looked wonderful. He wanted to put his arms around her and tell her how much he loved her but knew now was not the time. He would wait until they were rescued, and he could talk with her father. It was going to be difficult enough for people to believe they had not been immoral when they returned. He must be careful for it to remain true.

Tommy lifted his head and watched as Jed stuck his head in the doorway, alert for any danger to Lizzie. Jed smiled at the sight of the dog curled up in the corner of the kitchen, out of the way but close to her. Tommy had really taken to her, and he looked as if he had never been away from home, other than being so skinny. Lizzie dished a small chunk of bear fat from the pot and blew on it until cool before tossing it to Tommy, whose tail beat a tattoo on the floor. Tommy wasn't going to stay skinny long. Jed shook his head and walked back out to where he had the bear hide tacked to the wall. He grasped a scraper and began scraping the last of the fat and meat remnants from the skin.

CHAPTER 67

C harles rose from the table and slid Sue's chair back as she stood. "Come on, Jim. I want you to see something and meet some people before we leave tonight."

Charles put an arm around Jimmy and squeezed his shoulder as he took Sue's arm. He led the way from the dining room and down a hallway under an arch with a military crest and a sign stating "Company Hdqts. Members Only."

He pushed open a door and stepped aside for Sue to precede him. Several men seated on couches and overstuffed chairs stood to their feet and looked inquiringly at her until Charles and Jimmy followed her in.

"As you were," said Charles. "I want you all to meet Sue Jenson, the chief surgical nurse and anesthesiologist from Tokyo General when they put both me and James Romson back together. This is her son, Jim, who I want to meet some of you yahoos—although, for the life of me, I don't know why!" The men laughed as they all moved forward to introduce themselves to both Sue and Jimmy.

"I know it is not normal procedure, but I would like to nominate Sue Jenson as an honorary member of the Company. I brought it up to JC, who thought it a good idea." Charles turned to Sue. "This room is the club I told you this place belongs to. JC is our commandant for this year. Several men in the outfit were from the area, so when we got back from Vietnam, we started the club.

"It is open to all who served in our battalion but is primarily for Fox Company. All here tonight served in or with Fox Company during the Tet Offensive. No one is allowed in here other than members, except on family occasions. It is our place to escape to when memories or pressures are too great. Rooms are available for men from out-of-town, and you would be surprised how often they are in use. We look out for each other."

Jim looked at the men and around the room in wide-eyed astonishment.

"You see, when we returned home, no one wanted us. Even the VFW and the American Legion wouldn't accept Vietnam veterans, so we had no place to go, nowhere to belong. Most are in the Marine Corps League, but we wanted something a little more informal. We loosely patterned the club on the League, but very loosely. All club officers are elected each year, and rank has no bearing. Officers and enlisted men are equal in this room.

"We do accept some from other branches of the service, but for the most part all served in the Corps, as did all who are present tonight, except for Tran, here. He was a major in the ARVN, the Army of the Republic of Vietnam, and escaped after the fall of Saigon. James sponsored him when he immigrated and brought his family to the States."

More than one eye needed wiping before all the men introduced themselves to Sue and thanked her for her part in saving Charles and James. They represented a wide variety of backgrounds and careers, but all of them had fought together on a cut-off hilltop during one of the most ferocious battles of the war. To meet one of the medical people responsible for saving two of their number meant a lot to them.

"Jim, there is one other exemption to allow nonmembers into the room. The club is available to members' sons so they will have opportunity to learn from other members. You are not my son, but I requested a waiver to allow you to come in under my auspices, if you are interested." Sue looked at Jimmy out of the corner of her eye but said nothing.

Jimmy looked up at Charles, wide-eyed, and just nodded.

"Our purpose, Jim, is not to make Marines of our children but to educate them on what really happened over there, to develop in them a love of country, and to demonstrate the camaraderie we have developed."

"Coffee, Charles?" one of the men asked. "Sue? Would you like something, Jim?" Charles nodded and cups were brought over.

Jim spoke up for the first time. "Could I have coffee, too, please?" He glanced over at his mother, who, with a knowing look on her face, gave him a small smile and nodded.

"Certainly. Wouldn't want to leave you out. What are you in school this year? Freshman, sophomore?"

"I'm a freshman, sir."

"Hey, there, young man, we're all grunts here. 'Sir' is just for the brass. I'm just plain Smitty."

"Thank you, sir, but no. Mr. Charles has taught me respect. As far as I'm concerned 'sir' fits you. Maybe not in a military sense but for who you are and my relationship to you."

"Well, I'll be! Who would have thought the staff sergeant would have had so much sense to teach a kid! Son, you'll do all right. You keep listening to Charles, you hear me? As far as I'm concerned, you have my vote and proud to have you in the Company."

A number of the other men in the room agreed.

Sue looked at her son as if he were a stranger. She could not have been prouder of him. He was really growing up under Charles's influence.

Later, JC and Timmy entered together and went directly to Charles, Sue, and Jimmy. "Sue, I may call you Sue, mayn't I?" At her nod, JC went on. "I hope you enjoyed your dinner this evening. Charles likes to remember the old times once in a while. He said he especially wanted Jim to experience some of it and to meet up with some of the men from the Company. Normally, we don't bring in outsiders, but it's our intent to accept you both as family. Knowing your contributions to Charles and James, you are more than just a guest. We wish to make you, Sue, with the approval of the club, an honorary member of the Outriders Company. If you will come with me—you, too, young man—we will invest you into our organization."

With that, JC took Sue by the arm and led her to a small dais at the head of the room where they stood between the flag of the United States and the Marine Corps flag. Timmy followed along behind, walking with Jimmy.

"I call the Company to order," called JC. Instantly, all the men popped to attention. Anywhere else, middle-aged men in suits and ties standing at attention would be odd, but here, somehow, it seemed appropriate.

"We have a quorum," reported Tran.

"Salute to the colors," called JC, and as one the men turned and faced the flag and together said the pledge of allegiance.

"Chaplain, take your place."

A slight, balding man stepped to the dais and, turning to the altar behind the flags, opened a large, well-used Bible and then faced the group. "Let us pray." He led them in prayer and stepped down from the dais.

"At ease, take your seats," said JC solemnly. With a slight rustle, the assembled men relaxed their postures and then sat down.

"Thank you all for making yourselves available for this unscheduled meeting. We are convened for a very special purpose. As I just told Sue, it is our intention to invest Sue Jenson as an honorary member of the Outriders Company. Are there any comments?" He paused momentarily. "Very well. I call the question. All in favor say 'Aye.'"

A chorus of "Ayes" sounded.

"Any opposed say 'Nay.'"

There was no response.

"Very good." JC gave Sue a quick smile and then faced the audience. He held out a hand, and Tran Nguyen, sergeant at arms, stepped onto the dais and extended a rolled parchment. JC unrolled the parchment, which was embossed with the company crest, and said solemnly, "Attention to orders: For services rendered, the Outriders Company hereby extends honorary inclusion in the Company to Captain Sue M. Jenson, RN, USNR Retired." JC then read the honorary membership proclamation with the accompanying citation describing her actions in caring for Charles and James. He turned to Sue and extended the rerolled parchment to her and shook her hand. "Little Timmy" Wright pinned a lapel pin with the company crest on her collar. Sue noted it was the same as the one on Charles's lapel and on the lapel of each of the men in the room.

JC then turned to Jim and said, "We are also extending, by special request, a 'Son' membership to James R. Thompson, under the auspices of Staff Sergeant Charles Sitton, USMC Retired. Jim, you qualify as the son of Captain Jenson, but Charles has requested for you a special 'Son' status, which we allow for young men without fathers in the home. Do you accept?"

Jim stood up as straight and tall as he was able and whispered, "Oh yes, sir! Thank you, sir."

JC shook his hand. "Welcome aboard." Tran extended another rolled parchment to JC, which he in turn gave to Jim, then JC shook his hand again. Little Timmy pinned a lapel pin to Jim's collar and shook his hand.

"Company, Atten-hut!" JC called, and the men again snapped to attention. "Dismiss." All the men took a step backward and resumed conversing among themselves. Several men gathered around Sue and Charles, among them Tran.

"Thanks for driving down for this, Tran. I appreciate it," said Charles.

"I would not have missed this for anything, Charles. Sue, I welcome you to the Outriders. Jim," he had caught Charles's change in address of Jimmy, "I'm glad to have you here, also. You will learn a lot from these men if you pay attention."

"Yes, sir, I will. That was awesome!"

"We like to remember our service and remind ourselves of why we served," Tran said. "It is very easy for those who have never had their freedoms threatened or have not served and paid the price to take their freedom lightly. I never do, nor will I, for I know what freedom costs. For me, to have become an American citizen after the war made it that much more special.

"Now, if you will please excuse me. I hate to run off, but, unlike one whose name won't be mentioned, some of us have to be at work tomorrow." He laughed as he clapped Charles on the shoulder, winked at Jim, and shook Sue's hand. Charles, a wry grin on his face, just shook his head.

JC and Timmy walked over to Jimmy. "Jim, I'm glad you are here. I know Charles thinks a lot of you and your mom. He talks about you all the time. Right, JC?"

"You got that straight! Jim, we want you to see some things while you're here. You will find we don't talk much about what went on over there. For some of us, the memories are just too painful, and we do all we can to forget. We will sometimes tell stories among ourselves, and you are welcome to listen in if you hear us talking, but asking questions is not considered polite—unless someone offers, that is. Understand?"

"Yes, sir."

"Each one of these men—and I hope you get acquainted with each of them—has seen combat and knows what it is to be absolutely terrified but to go on and do his job anyway. Many times in your life you will be scared. There is no shame in being scared. Any man who does not get frightened is either a fool or insane. You don't want to be around those. True bravery is not being unafraid but being afraid and doing the job anyway."

Before the evening ended, each of those men from the Outriders Company took the time to introduce himself to Jimmy and to tell a little bit about his connection with the Company. It was a somber-eyed and thoughtful young man who walked from the club room.

Sue, in turn, was overwhelmed by the reception she received. Smitty called out to her as they left, "Sue, you be sure and come back, now! You don't have to bring the staff sergeant if you don't want!" which generated laughter in the room. Sue grabbed Charles's hand tightly and waved it back at Smitty with a smile on her face.

Sue kissed Charles's cheek as he opened the car door for her.

"Thank you. This has been a wonderful evening." She recognized Charles had opened a door into his life that had been closed to her, and almost everyone else, before now. She knew their relationship had deepened.

"The food was wonderful, and your friends are amazing. They are closer to each other than brothers!"

"Indeed. Henry V's line gets overused all the time, but it is true. *For he to-day that sheds his blood with me Shall be my brother. . . .*"

Sue squeezed Jimmy's hand. "Jimmy, I can't believe how much you have grown up in the last few months! Or shall I call you Jim?" She glanced at Charles before looking back at Jimmy again.

"I like the sound of Jim. It sounds more grownup. Thank you, Mr. Charles. I learned a lot tonight. Can we come back again?"

"Even if you have to wear a suit?"

Jim grinned and nodded.

"You can count on it, Jim. You can count on it."

CHAPTER 68

Detective Summers walked into the police department with a spring in her step that had been lacking for some time. She felt like she had a breakthrough in the Romson case, and she couldn't wait to discuss it with Chief Washington to determine where to go from here. She also looked forward to calling the Romsons and Charles Sitton to give them the news and discuss the possibilities with them. She knew they certainly deserved some hope.

After bringing the chief up to speed on her discoveries and calling the local FBI special agent with whom she had been working, she finally had the time she had been looking forward to, to call the parents. The day, which began with such promise, turned disappointing when she called both homes and then Romson Industries. The Romsons were out of town and would not return until the following week, and Charles Sitton was taking a few days off.

CHAPTER 69

The first of December did not bode well for Jed and Lizzie. The fall had been mild, which Jed appreciated very much since it allowed him time to gather nuts, do more hunting and fishing, and cut firewood for the ravenous fireplace, cookstove, and pot-bellied stove. The mild weather had ended two days before as a powerful nor'easter pummeled them with freezing rain. Over six inches of snow followed, blown and drifted by high winds howling through the trees and around the eaves of the lodge. The temperature hovered around ten degrees Fahrenheit, but with the wind chill factor it was about minus-forty. There was no way he wanted to go outside! He had carried in several days' worth of wood, but it was disappearing quickly, for no warmer than the lodge felt.

When Jed had come in with the last armload of wood, Lizzie had met him with a cup of acorn "coffee" and a warm smile.

"It's brutal out there! That wind will freeze your face off if you aren't careful, and the snow on the ice is slick." Jed shrugged off his parka and peeled off his fleece face mask. Ice had formed where his breath froze on the mask, leaving icicles hanging from his chin.

"Thanks for getting the wood, Jed."

He shrugged. "No problem." A shiver wracked his body. "Sure is a difference from last week, though. We had an easy fall, but it's going to be like this now for several months. Better get used to it."

Lizzie went back to grinding acorns to make a sort of flour. Jed had soaked the acorns thoroughly several times to blanch out the tannic acid, making them safe to eat. The water he saved to tan hides, which was much simpler than trying to keep water in a leaky, hollow oak stump.

Tommy, curled up at Lizzie's feet next to the cookstove, was warm and content.

Jed sipped on the acorn coffee, which was not the same as real coffee but wasn't bad. He had a pile of hickory nuts in front of him and a pail half full of empty shells on the floor. Hickory nuts were not easy to shell, but he thought they were quite good; plus they had a lot of nutritive value.

Overall, Jed was pleased with the amount of food stocked up for the winter. The mild fall had been very helpful; plus the bear added almost two hundred pounds to their larder. Getting some fresh meat now and then would be good for variety. The lake should be frozen sufficiently to start ice fishing within a few days. The cold weather also would now allow them to freeze their food, so drying and smoking would not be needed until the spring thaws. He knew they were very fortunate in having enough laid by.

"Once this nor'easter lets up I'll go out and see if I can scare up another deer. It'd be nice to get some fresh meat for a bit instead of just the dried stuff or that bear." Enforced idleness inside chafed at Jed, but Lizzie hoped it stayed cold for a few days. She enjoyed his presence in the lodge.

CHAPTER 70

etective Summers was frustrated. The file on the Romson-Sitton disappearance was officially going into the cold files today. No matter what possible lead she followed, there had been nothing. Every time she thought there was something, it turned into a dead end. It was as if they were swallowed by a black hole. All of her hopes following the Minnesota trip had been snuffed out.

The only good thing from her trip had been her growing friendship with Dan Hixon. They talked on the phone at least once a week, and he was scheduled to come to town to interview with James Romson for the company pilot job this weekend, although the hiring was basically a done deal. All that had to be done was to agree on a salary amount and find a plane.

The Beaver she had helped capture and confiscate in Minnesota was coming up for auction, and James and Dan were going to St. Paul to take a look at it. Since Dan was also an A&P mechanic, he could provide a good evaluation. The best part to Sarah was that she was going to dinner with Dan on Friday evening after his interview. She felt giddy like a schoolgirl again.

CHAPTER 71

The Romsons were decorating their house for Christmas, but their hearts weren't in it. As Jed had gotten older, decorating wasn't as exciting, but with him gone it seemed they were just going through the expected motions. Certainly they would celebrate Jesus' birth. Celebrating Jesus' birth never got old, but the rest of the festivities just seemed empty and hollow.

Their excitement over Detective Summers's find in Minnesota and what she had learned from Dan Hixon had long since faded. As with everything else surrounding the case, it all turned up empty. In their low moments, it seemed they would never see Jed again.

Dan Hixon was the only bright point James had, and James looked forward to meeting him on Friday. Their discussions over the telephone and Dan's experience and credentials were very positive. Dan seemed to fit the needs for a new pilot and was ready to accept a blend of corporate work with the limited bush work needed. His A&P skills were a big plus. Keeping maintenance on the plane in-house would save a significant amount of money and would allow for a higher pay scale to make it worthwhile for him to make the move. On Monday, the two of them would fly to St. Paul to take a look at the confiscated Beaver before the auction on Tuesday. The only drawback to their trip was they had to fly commercial, which James hated.

CHAPTER 72

Charles Sitton found himself with mixed emotions. While he missed Elizabeth terribly, his growing relationship with Sue and his friendship and mentorship of Jimmy was filling the void in his life caused by the loss of his wife. He found himself actually looking forward to Christmas. He had picked out a nice gift for Sue that sparkled, and he hoped, with expectation, she would accept it. He just wished Elizabeth could be there. The ache in his heart for her never seemed to go away, no matter what else was going on.

For Jimmy, he picked out a nice rifle. Charles had been teaching him firearm safety and the proper care of a weapon, and he felt Jimmy was ready to own his own rifle. Sue was hesitant at first, but when Charles took her to the firing range along with Jimmy, and she saw how careful Jimmy was, she consented to Charles's gift. She still thought Charles spoiled them, but Charles enjoyed having someone with whom to share his life.

For the first of December, it was a very nice day, so Charles and Jimmy were busy stringing Christmas lights around the eaves of the

Jenson home. Charles wasn't decorating at his house, not even a tree. With Elizabeth gone it seemed pointless, and he was spending Christmas with Sue and Jimmy anyway.

CHAPTER 73

Jed was having a tough time getting enough alone time to work on his gift for Lizzie. Since his bunk was in the open area, he didn't have a room where he could go alone to work on the gift. Without Lizzie noticing what he was doing, he had extracted all of the claws when he skinned the bear. He carefully bored small holes in the base of each claw and was stringing them on a finely braided, very thin rawhide necklace. It would not be Tiffany's, but it would be one of a kind and hopefully something memorable she would treasure. One way he tried to hide what he was doing was by carving a crèche for the mantel. When Lizzie saw him sitting back on his bunk working on little stuff, she thought that was what he was doing.

She nearly caught him one day. "Let's go see what Jed's doing, Tommy," he heard.

Almost frantically, Jed tucked the necklace and loose claws under his leg and picked up his knife and a half-finished donkey.

"Ooh. I like it." Lizzie leaned over his bunk and picked up a sheep. "How did you learn to carve like this?"

Lizzie sat down on his bunk by him and watched as he carefully crafted the donkey.

"Oh, it's easy enough." Jed looked up at Lizzie and winked, his heart warmed by her praise and having her close by. "I just try to do like Michelangelo said when he carved an angel. 'I just cut away anything that doesn't look like an angel.' "

"I like it."

"Thanks." Jed looked up to see Lizzie looking into his eyes and his heart fluttered. Suddenly, being cooped up in the lodge didn't seem as bad any longer.

Lizzie had managed to slip one of the coonskins out of the fur pile from Jed's snares without him noticing. She painstakingly worked it to make it very soft and pliable, even to the point of treating the hide the way squaws did, chewing some of the edges where she had trouble softening them. When it was softened to her satisfaction she crafted a coonskin cap for him to wear in the cold weather. She would have liked to have made him a beaver hat as had been popular years ago. However, there were only a couple of beaver pelts in the pile, and she didn't think she could get one without him noticing.

Shoes had become an issue. Jed had taken to making moccasins and wearing them when out, but with the colder weather they were difficult to keep warm. He had lined some with fur, which felt soft and warm, but they weren't totally satisfactory either. The last pairs he had made were long and came up to the knees. These were for walking in snow, but keeping the feet warm was an issue. He was going to have to experiment some more.

CHAPTER 74

After wrangling with the insurance company for months on end, James Romson and Bernie Watson finally came to an agreement with them on the replacement of the Romson Industries plane. Neither could believe it had taken over seven months to receive a check for the value of the lost aircraft, less a healthy deductible. The day the check cleared the bank, James changed insurance companies. He felt the years of business with no claims, plus the obvious theft of their aircraft, should have prompted the company to be more responsive, but they had not budged. The lack of an aircraft hampered testing on several new items under development. Chartering a plane and pilot had proven to be prohibitively expensive, so they had had to wait.

The only silver lining in that black cloud was the availability of the confiscated drug plane coming at the same time as the insurance settlement. After carefully checking it out with Dan Hixon, James promptly bid on the Beaver. Even though the plane came with notification from the DEA stating it was a confiscated drug plane, many bidders were afraid of being inspected and trace amounts of drugs being found. This kept the price of the plane well below market value and allowed for some very nice upgrades to be added. Since the Beaver was located in St. Paul anyway, James and Dan took the time to go over to Wipaire, Inc., one of the premier aircraft modification companies in the country. Dan Hixon felt like a kid who had been given the candy store, not just allowed inside. His experience as a bush pilot didn't tempt him into making the plane fancy, but he added top-of-the-line avionics and performance-enhancing options instead.

The hard part was determining what had to be done right away and what could be put off until later so the plane could be put into service more quickly. Fortunately, the wheels and skis from the old Beaver would fit the new one. Dan Hixon ordered parts and stockpiled them in the hangar where he promptly began installing some of the new equipment. Upgraded avionics and radios were the first things to happen. The plane would get a new paint job, in the company colors, but the paint would wait until spring.

Dan also purchased new, more aerodynamic Wipline floats to increase airspeed by over twenty miles per hour and decrease fuel consumption. He also made modifications to the wings to provide more lift and better airflow.

James finally had to make him take a couple of days off around Christmas. "Look, I appreciate you are trying to get the plane airworthy right away, but I'd rather have you fresh and ready when I need you. I don't need you burning out on me before we even get the plane in the air."

"Okay, boss. Would it be all right if I pick which days I want off?"

"I guess. Why?"

"I'll try to match them up with Sarah's off days. Maybe we can do something together."

"Sarah?"

"Yeah, Sarah Summers."

"Detective Summers?"

"Yeah. Cool, huh?"

James gave him a grin. "Go for it, Tiger. I just want you to take at least two days off between now and New Year's besides the holidays. I don't care which ones, and they don't count as vacation days either. I'll count them as comp time. I know for a fact you haven't been clocking all your hours. Being on salary doesn't mean I want to abuse you. You are already doing much more than I ask of you."

"Works for me. Thanks, boss. I think I'll have everything done shortly after the first. Unless you want skis put on. They will take me another week."

"I think we should do that. We need to take some people up to the lodge for some of the new product trials. I'm sure the lake is close to frozen if it isn't already. I'll get someone to give me a report on conditions next week."

CHAPTER 75

harles Sitton picked Jim up at the high school when school let out. They were going to the range to do a little target practice, but Charles's real purpose was to find out Jim's reaction to Charles's proposal to his mother. His stomach felt like he had butterflies, and he just couldn't get them to fly in formation. This was as bad as when he had had to talk to Collette's father all those years ago. He didn't need Jim's approval, but he really wanted it. The last thing he wanted to do was cause problems in the family.

"Hey, Mr. Charles!" Jim popped the door open and jumped in the Oldsmobile. He waved at a couple of guys who were watching them leave.

"Had an interesting day in school today. I told a couple of guys I couldn't play basketball tonight because we are going shooting. Mr. Swenson overheard us and went ballistic! He started ranting about how guns are evil and war is wrong and stuff like that. He got a big hubbub going in class. I don't care what he thinks. He's kind of weird anyway, but several of the guys asked if you would teach them to shoot. Could you do it?"

"I don't know. That is a lot of responsibility. I'm teaching you because I can keep an eye on you and make sure you do it right, and you won't do stupid stuff with a gun when I'm away from you. Guns are not toys! They can be fun to shoot and stuff, but you always have to remember they are tools, and they have to be respected accordingly. I wouldn't give a power saw to a kid to play with, and a gun can be as dangerous. I would have to think seriously about it and talk with their parents first to be sure they were on board with me teaching their sons."

"Cool! Would you? I told Jason I would ask you."

"Let me think about it for a few days. Tell them not to go out and buy a gun! . . . Tell you what. You can talk with the boys, but tell them they have to have their dads call me if their dads are okay with it. I'll not teach anyone unless I talk with his dad first. I have an idea convincing the mothers will be a little different." Charles paused, obviously thinking. "Also, I'm going to require the fathers to be there for at least the first session."

They pulled up at the range and got out of the car. As they unloaded the gun cases from the trunk, Jim said, "I think that will work. You might even be able to charge them something for teaching them."

"No. I'll not charge anything if I decide to do it. They will have to pay for their own ammo and will be responsible for cleaning the guns to my satisfaction, but I'll not charge them."

Jim impulsively gave Charles a hug, something he was not accustomed to doing. "Thanks. You're pretty cool, you know?"

"Thank you. I appreciate that." Charles took a deep breath. Now was as good a time as any. "Before we go in, I need to talk with you about Christmas. Will you keep a secret?"

"Of course!"

"I want your opinion on something, and I want you to be totally honest. Can you do that?"

"Sure. What's up?"

"Look. I bought a ring for your mother. She has come to mean an awful lot to me, and I want to ask her to marry me. I don't have to have your permission, but I would like to know you don't have a problem with it. I don't want to break up your family."

"Are you kidding me? It's the best news I've heard in a long time!" He threw both arms around Charles's neck. "Does that mean I get to call you Dad?"

Charles had to swallow and wipe a tear from the corner of his eye. "I don't know anything I would like better, son, but you'd better wait until it's official."

"Oh, geez. I hope I don't let it slip to Mom!"

CHAPTER 76

Footing outside the lodge was treacherous. The good news was the freezing rain had not been prolonged, and very few branches were down as a result, but the ice under the six inches of snow created a deceitfully slippery subsurface. Jed tread cautiously as he made his way to the woodpile, grabbed an armload of logs, and worked his way back in the door. Since the wind died down, it wasn't as cold, with the thermometer hovering at five degrees. On his second trip, he took the bucket full of hickory nut shells and spread them on the path to the woodpile. They helped a bit, but he still had to be cautious. To break a leg or sprain an ankle could be a death sentence at these temperatures. For sure, he would be staying close to the lodge.

Lizzie experimented with the acorn flour she had so painstakingly ground. It was grainy and nothing like wheat flour, but she was determined to be creative. The end result she fried on a griddle like pancakes. The pancakes turned out more like hard tortillas than pancakes, but with some of the blueberry preserves she had made in the summer, Jed liked them; it was all the confirmation Lizzie needed. Her love for Jed seemed to grow stronger every day. She longed to be able to express herself, but she knew she had to wait. It seemed all her life was about waiting!

Jed and Lizzie had just finished eating lunch when Jed heard an airplane in the distance. Instantly, he ran out the door, not even thinking to put on a coat. He slipped and fell hard, but was up quickly. An airplane was coming their way, but it wasn't a float plane, nor did it have skis. Jed knew it couldn't land, but he waved both arms above his head, hoping he would be seen. The pilot waggled his wings and kept on flying. Feeling the cold now that the excitement was over, Jed made his way, shivering, back into the lodge. Whether or not the pilot would report their presence, he had no idea, but for the first time in a long time he had hope. It might be only December second, but being discovered would be the best Christmas present he could ask for, and he didn't even mind if it came early.

Impulsively, Jed picked Lizzie up in his arms and danced her around the room.

CHAPTER 77

I n accordance with James's orders, Dan was taking a couple of days off work, but he was not exactly doing so in a manner James would have approved. He was flying his own Piper Tri-Pacer airplane, lovingly restored to its original condition, down to repainting it in its original pale washed-out mauve color scheme. Dan loved the old Tri-Pacer. The first time he had gone up in an airplane was when he was eight years old, and he had flown in a Tri-Pacer that looked just like this one. The Tri-Pacer was one of the last commercially built planes with a fabric wing instead of aluminum, and it was one of the first with a tricycle landing gear instead of a tailwheel.

Sarah thought Dan was showing off a little as he pre-flighted the plane, and she walked along with him. He pulled and wiggled and checked every little thing before saying it looked like it was safe to wind up the rubber bands. After climbing into the airplane and cinching the seatbelt snug against her waist, she asked, "Hey, what was with all the looking and wiggling and pushing and pulling on stuff before we got in?"

"Every pilot who wants to be an old pilot does that every time. I don't care if he just got out of the plane and then got back in. When you get it up in the air, there isn't a place to pull off the side of the road like you can with a car. You always check everything before taking off."

"I thought you were just showing off or something."

"Nope. You do it every time, and you do it the same way every time to be sure you don't forget something. The time you don't check may be the time something breaks. Flying isn't something I like to show off with. I know some guys do aerobatics and stuff, but they have planes built for doing that stuff. Never saw much use in it myself."

Sarah Summers sat in the right seat, enthralled by the view. She had flown commercially, but the view from the front, out the windscreen, was different from what she could see out a little porthole on the side of a jet. She held the yoke and had her feet on the rudder pedals, "following through," as Dan flew the craft. At first, the dials and gauges confused her, but they started making sense as Dan explained each one.

They were flying to another town for the day, about an hour's air time away. Because she was a police officer, Sarah was not comfortable going out much in her hometown. Too many people knew she was a cop, and she often wondered about her food or drinks. She had a few places she frequented that she trusted, but those weren't special for a date. Dan, being a pilot and having a plane, made going out of town for a fun day a lot easier.

"You have the airplane," Dan said with a smirk on his face.

"What?" Sarah almost yelled. "I'll crash us!"

"No, you won't. I'm right here. Just move the yoke around a little to get a feel for what it does. Easy, there. You can't pull it up quite so fast. This little thing won't handle it. Make your turns nice and easy. See, it's not so bad. Sort of like driving in 3-D." Dan took hold of the yoke for a minute to get them back on a straight and level flight.

"Here, you take it again. See if you can keep it straight and level for a little bit. See that barn out there a ways? Try to fly straight at it."

Sarah tensely held the yoke like it was trying to get away from her.

"Take it easy there. I don't want fingerprints implanted in the yoke," he said with a grin. He pointed at the altimeter, which was winding down.

"See the altimeter? You need to pull us back up a little bit. When I said fly straight at the barn, I didn't mean into it."

He softened his words with a smile. "You're doing fine. Relax. Hold the yoke like you would a steering wheel, and just handle it softly."

Dan pointed out the turn and bank indicator. "Just like you check your dash in the car, you need to check these instruments when flying. Check them a little more frequently than you would in a car. This one tells you if you are turning or not flying level. Also, keep an eye on your altimeter. It is easy to have a landmark, like that barn, and be following it and going down."

By the time they reached their destination, Sarah felt a lot more comfortable with control of the airplane. They were landing at a small uncontrolled airport, which was all the small city needed.

Dan said, "I'll take it back now and land it. You did well for a first time. See the airport?"

Sarah looked and looked but did not see anything that looked to her like an airport. It wasn't until Dan pointed it out to her that she could make it out.

"Things look a lot different from up here, don't they?"

"Um-hmm. Being up in the air like this puts things into perspective. What we think is big and important shows up for what it really is from the air—very small."

Sarah was pensive as a thought tugged at the back of her mind. She couldn't get a grip on what—but knew somehow it was important.

CHAPTER 78

Mary sat at her kitchen table with a cup of coffee and her open Bible in front of her. She struggled with depression over Jed's absence, especially with Christmas at hand. Thanksgiving had been tough. What was there to be thankful for? Now Christmas, her once favorite season, left her with a sour taste in her mouth. Desperately, she was reading through her Bible, looking for some encouragement. God had never failed her yet, nor did she think He would fail her now. It was the not knowing that left her hurting. If she knew the kids were dead, she would deal with it, but being in limbo hurt. From her Bible reading, Mary knew David had troubles multiple times in his life. She found comfort in the Psalms, particularly the ones David wrote.

Mary got up from her chair when she heard the garage door opening. James walked in the door and gave her a hug. He could tell Mary was struggling not to cry. "Don't worry, hon. I think we'll get him back."

"Are you sure? Have you heard anything?"

"No. I haven't heard anything you haven't. I just have a feeling he's still out there. Just hang on, and trust God."

CHAPTER 79

James was in the middle of a meeting with Tran and various department heads, trying to determine which of the new products needed to be on the first plane to the lodge, for testing, when Anh stuck her head in the door.

"Mr. Romson, I know you didn't want to be interrupted, but I have a Dave Henson on the phone from the Maine Department of Inland Fisheries and Wildlife. He said he's returning your call."

"Great! Please put him through." He pointed to Tran. "You guys work it out while I talk with Dave. That's what I put you in charge for. I'll back whatever you decide."

Picking up his phone, he said, "Hi, Dave. Thanks so much for getting back to me."

"Hi, James. I was out of town last week, and I'm trying to catch up. Sorry I missed your call. What can I do for you?"

"I'm looking for a condition report up at our lake. Is it frozen over enough to use skis, or can I get in with floats still?"

"No, you certainly can't use floats. I'm not sure about the ice yet. We just had a nor'easter hit, and it was cold, with about six inches of snow in Caribou, so you probably got about the same. Based on the forecasts, I think I'd wait until the first to try to get a plane in there, just to be on the safe side. You could maybe get one in now if it was light. What's up? Are you coming up to get your people for Christmas?"

"Get my people?"

"Haven't you had a team up there since the summer? I flew over there the other day—let's see . . . it was the second—when I went up to the conference, and a long-haired guy with a beard waved at me. I just figured he was one of yours."

James's heart leaped into his throat. Could it be Jed? *Dear God, please!*

"No, we haven't had a team up there. My plane was stolen, and my son and Charles's daughter were kidnapped. We've had no means of going to the lodge. I wonder if it could be Jed and Elizabeth! Any chance you will have anyone in the area? Could you check it out for me?"

"I'm sorry. Unless it is an emergency, I don't have any way to get there before the first of the year. We have just a skeleton crew between now and New Year's Day. Is it an emergency?"

"I guess I couldn't call it an emergency, unless you think the guy you saw was in distress."

"No, he looked okay to me. He wasn't acting like he was trying to signal an emergency, just waving. Some of those guys out there get excited to see anybody."

"All right. We are planning a trip up there anyway. We'll check them out. Thanks for your help." With a shaking hand, James hung up. He became aware of the silence in the office as everyone looked at him.

"Dave Henson said there has been someone at the lodge all summer. Do you think maybe it's Jed?"

Everyone started talking at once, excited at the possibility. James's mind was in a whirl. Quickly, he picked up the phone and buzzed his secretary.

"Anh, I don't care what either of them is doing. I want Charles and Dan Hixon in my office just as soon as they can possibly get here. . . . No, I'll tell you later. Just get them here for me right now!"

James took over the meeting. "Everybody, pipe down. Here is what we are going to do. I know tomorrow is Christmas Eve, and I don't want to get in the way of family plans, but if you have any time available, I want it. We will decide what is ready to go north right now, and as soon as Charles and Dan get here we will determine how quickly we can get the plane ready, and we will go. I'm sure Mary will want to go, as will Charles, and of course me, so you work out who else is going up to do the tests. This may interfere with the New Year's holiday, so keep that in mind. I'll leave it to you to decide how much weight is available for product and personnel. Have the report ready for me before you go home tonight. I don't know how soon we can have the plane ready, but as soon as it is ready it will be loaded and will take off. Dan will be here shortly, and we will know the timetable."

The office door burst open and Charles hurried in. "What's wrong, James? Anh said it was an emergency."

"No, no emergency. Grab a chair." James waited until Charles was sitting before saying, "Dave Henson just called me from up in Maine, returning my call. Somebody has been staying in the lodge all summer. Said he was outside waving at the plane when it went over."

"Jed?" Charles was halfway out of his seat.

"We don't know, and Dave doesn't have anyone he can send to check until after New Year's because of the holidays. We'll have the plane ready before then. I'm trying not to get my hopes up. I don't know if I could take it if it's someone else."

"Call Dan and see how quickly he can get the plane together!"

"Anh called him right after she called you. I expect him here in just a few minutes. We'll take the plane up there just as soon as we can get it off the ground. I know you'll want to go along."

"Absolutely! I'll go out to the hangar and help Dan. I can turn a wrench and put the skis on as well as he can. He can finish up the electronics while we get the rest of it put together. Can I have a couple of my guys?"

"Are you kidding? I already told these yahoos I need them tomorrow if it won't interrupt family stuff. Now, I've got to call Mary before Dan gets here. You call your guys, and get them ready to roll. Double-time if they want to work late tonight and tomorrow, but make sure it doesn't mess with their family plans."

"That won't be a problem. My guys all love Elizabeth and keep asking what they can do. Let me call Sue. Any chance I could take her and Jim along?"

"Works for me. Hey, Tran, we have others going up with us. Figure that . . ." James thought out loud. "We may just have to go up empty and send the stuff up later. . . . In fact, that's what we will do! You guys belay the planning. Put something together for after New Year's. That way it doesn't have to be rushed. Let's hold off this meeting until next week. Any of you who have the time to help, we'll head out to the hangar after Dan gets here. If you have plans with your families, those plans come first! If you want to go ahead and take off now, feel free."

All of the men cleared out of the office and hurried to their own offices and phones to cancel whatever plans they had for the evening and to try to rearrange whatever they could for Christmas Eve in order to be in on getting the plane in the air as soon as possible.

James called Mary. "Honey, are you sitting down? Now, don't get your hopes up too much, but I just talked with Dave Henson from up at Fisheries in Maine. He said someone has been staying in the lodge all summer. He thought we had a team up there. . . . No, I don't know if it's

Jed. . . . No, he can't send anyone unless we declare an emergency. Most of his staff are off for the holidays. . . . Yes, we are working on that right now. Dan is on his way; he just walked in. I'm going to find out how fast we can get the plane in the air. . . . Of course, you can go! I gotta go. I'll let you know just as soon as I know something. . . . Okay, come ahead if you want. Better yet, why don't you go to the hangar? Pick up several pizzas on the way. I have an idea we are going to have an army trying to put the plane together! . . . Love you, too!"

Charles was on another phone with Sue. "No, honey, I don't know if it's Elizabeth or not. We're going to talk with Dan Hixon now and see how soon we can get the plane in the air. Do you think Jim would want to go? . . . Yes, I'd like to take you both. I'll call you when I know more. . . . Yes, we'll be at the hangar late, and I'm going to have to take a raincheck on tomorrow also. . . . Sure, if you want to come, you can. Why don't you stop at Kentucky Fried and pick up a couple of buckets. I'll pay you back. . . . No, I don't really know how many will be there, but I think we are going to have several trying to help. . . . Love you, too, honey."

"Hey, Dan. Did James tell you what is going on yet?"

"No, I didn't. I was waiting for you to get off the phone. Dan, here's the deal. We just heard from Maine that someone has been in the lodge all summer. They thought we had a crew up there, so no one checked on them. Either it's Jed and Elizabeth, or someone has been squatting. Fisheries said because of the holidays they don't have anyone they can send up there unless it is an emergency. Here's the question: How quickly can we get the plane operational if we pitch in? Charles says his guys will all help, and I had the department heads in here. I told them not to come if they have family stuff, but I know they will be there."

Dan thought for a few minutes, jotting notes on a pad of paper. "I can put off some of the avionics stuff I wanted to upgrade, and a couple of other things really don't have to be done now. The plane is airworthy.

After all, it was operational when they nabbed it, and I flew it down here. The seats haven't come in yet."

"Call Wipaire and have the seats overnighted. I don't care what it costs."

"Okay. I can do that. Won't be able to get them before the twenty-seventh or the twenty-eighth. We have to pull the floats and install the wheels and skis. That is about forty man-hours. Doesn't take an A&P to do it; I just have to check them out. I think if we can work late tonight, and I can work on it tomorrow and maybe a little bit Christmas afternoon . . ."

"Belay that! Nobody works Christmas. That's final. One day won't make that much difference. It isn't like you are trying to get stuff in to the Ia Drang with the 7th Cav."[1]

"Okay, boss. I'll give you tomorrow, though. Depending on how much help I get, we should be able to make it the twenty-eighth or twenty-ninth depending on when we get the seats."

"Here's what we are going to do then. You head out to the hangar and lay out what has to be done, and plan for several hands. From the sound of things, we may have more than we can use, but everyone wants to help get the kids back." James fought back tears. "Anyway, Mary is going to pick up some pizzas and bring them out to the hangar for anyone who helps tonight."

Charles broke in. "Sue wanted to come out, too. I told her to pick up some KFC."

"All right." James chuckled. "At least we won't be hungry! Figure out what you need, Dan, and then call Charles at the plant. Any extra tools

---

1   For more on this, the first major battle in the Vietnam War involving American troops fighting the North Vietnamese Army, see General Hal Moore and Joe Galloway's excellent book *We Were Soldiers Once . . . And Young*. The Medal of Honor was awarded to Captain Ed Freeman and Captain Bruce Crandall for multiple volunteer flights carrying water and ammunition to the beleaguered troops and for carrying out the wounded when med-evac helicopters would not go in due to heavy enemy fire.

you want, he can bring with the guys who want to help. Actually, first I want you to call Wipaire right now and get those seats moving." James pointed to a phone. "Anything else you have on order you need now, get it in the same shipment. Charles, you get back to the plant, and get your end of things ready."

CHAPTER 80

Jed stumbled into the lodge, head down and shoulders slumped, just before sundown. He had walked his trap line of snares but had little success. The freezing rain had spoiled several, and snow had buried others. Wordlessly, he slumped onto the couch, tears stinging his eyes.

It had been a trying week all around. First of all, it had been the forced confinement indoors. It had been too bitterly cold to venture out more than he absolutely had to. Then there was the disappointment of thinking they had been discovered three weeks prior. He knew someone had to come sometime, but having his hopes dashed so close to Christmas was hard to take. Tomorrow was Christmas Eve, and he didn't believe in Santa Claus. Tonight, he and Lizzie would place the crèche on the mantel in preparation, but he was having trouble getting into the spirit of things.

Lizzie, on the other hand, enjoyed having Jed around the lodge so much. She knelt down in front of him and pulled his fur-lined moccasins from his feet and then looked up into his eyes. "It's going to be all right, Jed."

Jed nodded his head slightly, but his heart wasn't in it.

Lizzie sat facing him on the couch, with one knee folded under her, and took his hand in hers. She rubbed his hand, trying to get some warmth back into it.

"I kind of like it with us alone together like this." A little smile crossed her lips as she reached across Jed to capture his other hand so she could warm it. "I know you thought we were going to get to go home for Christmas, and I wish we could, too, but if we did, it wouldn't be us having Christmas together." She lifted his hand to her lips and placed a little kiss in his palm. "I like being with you like this."

Lizzie had spent quite a bit of time alone for the last several months as Jed was out cutting wood, hunting, fishing, and running his snares. To have him all to herself, even if he was working on pelts or whittling the crèche, was special. Her love for him was growing more than she thought possible. She had wondered how two people could love each other so much and what they would find to talk about, but she was having no trouble.

When Jed came in the door, she was there to meet him with a fresh cup of acorn coffee and supper almost ready to put on the table. She, too, had been excited when the plane flew over, but she really didn't expect them to come back with all the snow on the ground and the lake freezing over. After all, where would they land? Besides, they were probably used to seeing people wave as they went past.

Jed let loose a big sigh and wiped the tears from his eyes. "I'm sorry, Lizzie. I love spending the time with you, too. I just hoped to be home for Christmas. I'm just being a big baby, but I miss Mom and Dad." Had he stopped to think about it, he would have been surprised at the role reversals in the time between their kidnapping and now. He was homesick, and Lizzie had made a home.

CHAPTER 81

Sarah Summers got the news from Dan that he would not be able to go to dinner with her that evening. He was going to be working on the plane on Christmas Eve also. At first she was disappointed, angry even. After reflection, though, she realized she was reacting the same way her ex-husbands had when she was forced to work a case when they had things planned. But it was part of police work—the long hours, the missed dinners, the waiting for her to finally come home—only to be so exhausted she just crashed on the bed. This was different, but the circumstances demanded the same.

Sarah jumped in her car and drove to the hangar to spend what time she could with Dan there. She was surprised at the crowd of people who wanted to get the plane going to see if it was the kids at the lodge. When she saw Mary and Sue, she quickly helped with setting food out for the people working. Then Sarah got back into her car and went to the police department and borrowed the large coffeepot from the emergency truck. Knowing the chief's friendship with James, she knew it would not be an issue if the matter came up at all.

CHAPTER 82

When Dan Hixon walked into the hangar, he found several men already there, waiting for instructions. Charles had arrived first and was rigging the crane overhead so they could remove the floats. He had obviously changed floats for skis before, so Dan left him alone until James walked in about fifteen minutes later. When Dan saw James, he called Charles over so he could talk with them together.

"When I told the parts guy at Wipaire what we were doing and what the rush was, he said he wouldn't send the stuff overnight. He is loading it on one of their Beavers and is going to fly it down here first thing in the morning on his own time! He just asked if you would cover his fuel. He's really hoping you get your kids back."

James couldn't help it. After all the stress, the hopes, the dashed hopes, the time spent praying prayers that didn't seem to be heard, he broke down in tears.

All of these people were here on their own time when they could have been with their families, and now this news put him over the tipping point. Charles, also overwhelmed, embraced James, and the two of them shed tears together. With all the extra help and the seats coming so quickly, it looked like they would be able to leave the day after Christmas if, that is, they thought the ice would be strong enough.

Dan put a couple of the plant maintenance men who were adept with tools in charge of non-maintenance workers who were willing but not as knowledgeable. Then he assigned them the task of finishing the rigging and lifting of the plane. Once the plane was off the floor, they would remove the floats. Setting up a ladder to give him access to the plane cabin, Dan climbed in and began putting the control panel back together. Fortunately, he had not yet disconnected any of the gauges or controls themselves.

James and Charles both climbed into the cabin by way of the ladder and asked what they should do.

"Probably the best thing for you two would be to start with a couple of shop vacs, cleaning the marijuana residue out. The DEA cleaned it pretty well, but I can still smell some of it on board, and I'd be more comfortable with all residue gone. Dating a detective wouldn't keep me out of jail if the wrong person wanted to inspect. They couldn't keep me, but there is no point in spending any time in a local jail until you can bail me out."

He stuck his head out of the cockpit window. "Hey, Sarah!"

When Sarah looked up to see what he needed, Dan beckoned her over to the aircraft. "Could you climb up here and assist James and Charles with cleaning out any residue? I don't want to go to jail while I'm waiting for you to bail me out."

"Be right up. Let me grab us some gloves first." Sarah jogged out to her squad car and retrieved some latex gloves for the three of them and then jogged back in to oversee and certify the cleanup.

By nine o'clock everything had been cleaned, the control panel reassembled, and the floats removed. Dan inspected the work done and approved it all, amazed so much had been done so quickly. It was a tired but satisfied crew who left the hangar, knowing they had done well.

As they were leaving, Dan stopped James.

"Look, boss, Sarah has sweat bullets on this case. There is one seat open since we aren't taking any freight. Would it be okay if I asked her if she wanted to go along? It might be a wild goose chase, but I have a feeling it's those kids. What do you say?"

"It's all right by me, but it is going to be a long flight up there and back."

"Thanks, boss. Means a lot to me. I'm pretty sure she wants to go but didn't feel she could ask."

CHAPTER 83

Jed woke up the morning of Christmas Eve to see snow falling quietly but steadily. There was no wind, and the view across the lake was almost ethereal.

As he often did, he made acorn coffee, but instead of getting ready to go out, he sat at the table and waited for Lizzie to wake up. When he heard her stirring, he poured her a cup and put honey in it.

Lizzie gave Jed a bright smile for so early in the morning. "Thanks. I didn't expect to see you still here."

"I decided not to go out today. There's really nothing I have to do except bring in a little wood. What would you like to do today?"

That earned Jed a wide smile. "I really get you all to myself all day?" Lizzie let out a happy sigh and reached across the table to squeeze Jed's hand. "Could we just have a quiet day where we don't have to do anything? Maybe shell some nuts, sing some Christmas songs, and play some games?"

"Sounds good to me, all except me singing."

Lizzie laughed and swatted Jed's hand lightly. "You have a good voice, and you know it." She lifted his hand and nestled it against her cheek. "I get to have you all day? I like that."

Jed had found and cut down a small cedar the day before, and they stood it in the corner opposite the fireplace. Of course, they had no lights for it and no decorations except for some popcorn Lizzie found in the pantry. Together, they popped it, and, with some thread from a sewing kit, they strung it together and draped the popcorn garlands on the tree. It gave an old-timey, Christmassy fragrance and feel to the room.

CHAPTER 84

S even o'clock Christmas Eve morning found James, Charles, and Dan at the hangar, preparing to install the landing struts and wheels. They did not expect as many people there to help since the men all had family responsibilities, but they knew a few would show up at least for a while. The hardest part was done, and the whole thing should be finished by evening.

Tran walked into the building carrying a couple boxes of doughnuts.

"Breakfast, guys! I just saw a float plane touch down out there. It might be your parts."

Dan hurried out the door as Charles and James each grabbed a doughnut and poured a cup of coffee.

Under James's guidance, Charles lowered the plane so they would not have to raise the struts so high in the air to fasten them to the fuselage. When it was to the level of Charles's satisfaction, he and James struggled to hold the strut up high enough to line the bolt holes as Tran tried to slip the first bolt into place. Once the first bolt was in, it would be easy enough to align the others. At last after several tries the first bolt slipped home. With a sigh of relief, Charles and James released their hold on the strut and stretched their backs.

The door swung open and Jim Thompson walked into the hangar. "Hey, Mr. Charles, a plane is taxiing to the landing. Mr. Dan is guiding him in."

"Great! Why don't you grab a doughnut and see what you can do to help him unload?"

Charles lifted the strut one more time, and Tran slipped the remaining bolts into their holes. Charles slipped the washers and nuts on loosely. They would leave them for Dan to tighten down and inspect. The three men moved to the right side and repeated the process. When the second strut was installed, Charles raised the crane once more and mounted the wheels on the struts.

Dan walked in the door with the visiting pilot. Charles and James both walked over and shook his hand wordlessly. Words would not come at the moment. The pilot, seeing their grief-stricken faces, understood and nodded at each. Three men from the plant walked in the door just then, and the three of them and Jim, working quickly, were able to unload the parts from the plane and release the pilot to return home to his family.

Charles and James both walked out to the plane and embraced the pilot, again wordlessly. Their gratitude was more than evident.

James handed him a check. "I think that will cover your fuel. Do something nice for your family with any leftovers."

"This isn't necessary."

"I didn't do it because it was necessary. I did it because it was right. I appreciate this more than you know."

"Thanks! You be sure to get those kids back. Merry Christmas!"

"It will be now, thanks to you! A Merry Christmas to you and your family as well." James shook the pilot's hand once more before the pilot turned and climbed into the plane, taxied out to clear water, and took off. As he flew back over, he wagged the wings in goodbye as James and Charles waved in return.

CHAPTER 85

Christmas morning dawned bright, clear, and sunny. Jed was in no hurry to do anything. He was struggling not to be depressed over being stranded on Christmas. He walked outside and carried wood into the lodge and filled the wood boxes while acorn coffee brewed. Lizzie, still not much of a morning person, wandered from her room and poured each of them a mug and added honey.

When Jed finished filling the wood boxes, he shrugged off his parka and gladly accepted the coffee. "It's cold out there!"

When they sat down for breakfast, they each pulled out their Bibles. Jed read the Christmas story from Luke and then also read Matthew's account. When they finished reading, Lizzie said, "Wait right there and close your eyes. I have something for you, but I didn't have any way to wrap it." She jumped from the table and scurried to her room. "No peeking!"

"I'm not."

Lizzie came back to the breakfast table and set the coonskin hat in front of Jed. "Okay, you can open your eyes now. Merry Christmas, Jed. I love you."

Jed opened his eyes and saw the hat. He picked it up. Full of wonder, he felt the fur and the softness of the skin. "How did you do this? The skin is so soft!"

Lizzie glowed with happiness. "I chewed the skin to make it soft like you told me squaws used to do. Did I do it right?"

"It's marvelous. Thank you! Now it's your turn. Close your eyes and don't peek." He got up from the table and walked to his bunk and came back with the necklace of bear claws.

Slipping up behind her, he said, "No peeking now." He draped the necklace around her neck. Gently gathering her hair, he tied the necklace beneath. "Now you can look." He knelt on one knee in front of her and said, "I don't have a diamond, but I love you. Will you marry me when we get home?"

"Oh, Jed! Yes! I'll never look at this without knowing you love me. I never doubted it."

She flung her arms around his neck, and he embraced her, satisfied. He would always remember this as his best Christmas ever.

CHAPTER 86

J ames and Mary had a quiet Christmas morning. They had agreed to find someone needy to give a gift to rather than to each other and just enjoyed spending the morning together. They, too, read the Christmas story as they had each Christmas of their marriage. The anticipation of the trip to Maine the next morning occupied their minds, but they had determined not to talk about the trip, nor whether it was Jed, today. Today they would spend appreciating the gift of the Savior. In the afternoon they would go over to Sue Jenson's home to have dinner with Sue, Charles, and Jim.

CHAPTER 87

harles woke up early in the morning and looked out his window to see the sun rising in a clear sky. Hoarfrost on the ground and trees sparkled like diamonds, making him think of the little package he had on the table for Sue. He felt as excited as if he were a little boy. He looked at his clock, willing it to go more quickly, wishing it was nine o'clock instead of only six so he could go to Sue's.

Finally, the clock ticked around to eight-twenty-five, and he couldn't take it any longer. He was afraid he would wear a path in his carpet as he paced back and forth, waiting to go. He would sit down for a couple of minutes and then get up and look at the clock, just knowing it had to be time, only to be disappointed again. He walked into the kitchen where he had Sue and Jim's gifts on the table to be sure they were where they were supposed to be, not realizing he had done exactly the same thing not five minutes before.

At eight-thirty, Charles slipped Sue's little box into his coat pocket and the larger box containing Jim's rifle under his arm and went out to the garage. He put Jim's box in the trunk, patted his pocket to be certain

Sue's package was still there, and got into his Oldsmobile. Hitting the garage door remote, he backed out to the street and drove as sedately as he could to Sue's house.

When he pulled into the driveway, Charles hesitated for a minute before getting out of his car, but he saw Sue open her door with a smile. Opening the trunk, Charles picked up Jed's rifle, then patted his pocket one more time to be certain of Sue's box before he walked to the door.

Sue gave him a big hug. "Merry Christmas, Charles. I won!"

"You won?"

Sue laughed. "I bet Jim you would be early. He said eight-forty-five, but I said eight-thirty-five." She looked at her watch. "It's eight-thirty-six."

Charles looked at her sheepishly. "I couldn't wait. I've been wearing out my carpet for an hour."

Sue giggled. "I've been waiting for you, too. I think you're sweet."

Jim bounced down the stairs. "Good morning, Mr. Charles! Merry Christmas!" He winked behind his mother's back. He hadn't slipped up.

Charles placed the box containing Jim's rifle under the tree but slipped Sue's box into his pants pocket when he hung up his coat.

After eating breakfast, they gathered in the living room and exchanged gifts. Jim was thrilled with his rifle, a Remington Model 700, chambered for a 30.06 cartridge. When all the other gifts had been passed out, Charles reached into his pocket and pulled out Sue's box. He handed it to her silently, and as she opened it, he dropped to one knee.

"Sue, you know I love you. You have become very important to me. Will you marry me?"

"Oh, Charles! It's beautiful!" Tears welled up in her eyes. "I want to say yes so badly, but I want to be sure your daughter is okay with me first. I don't want to do anything that would come between you two."

"I can assure you she will be more than happy. She has been after me to find someone for the last two years. Why don't you put it on, and we will see what she says?"

Jim broke in, "Mom, that's what Mr. Charles said to me when he asked if I had a problem with him marrying you. He didn't want to come between us." Softly, almost in a whisper, he said, "He told me I can call him Dad. I hope you will say yes."

CHAPTER 88

Jed was out early in the morning the day after Christmas. His new hat felt good on his head. Lizzie made it so he could wear it over his ears, where the fur was soft and warm. He was checking his snares, and although he did not expect to see any, he watched for a deer. He wanted some fresh meat since the temperature was cold enough to freeze the meat, and he would not have to smoke or jerk it. Overall, it had not been a very successful trip. Something had tripped several of his snares, but they had been empty. He did have two foxes and three raccoons, though.

Night came early this time of the year, so he had headed back toward the lodge to be certain he was able to make it before dark when he heard the plane. Walking as rapidly as he could in snowshoes, he broke out into the clearing by the lodge as the plane swept overhead. It was a Beaver, but one he had never seen before. Still, he waved wildly with both arms. The pilot waggled his wings and then flew low and slow over the lake before pulling up and circling over the lodge. Lizzie came out the door, hurriedly pulling on a parka as she came.

CHAPTER 89

D an Hixon saw the figure hurrying out of the trees as the plane approached the lodge. His first thought was of coming into an LZ for an extraction in Vietnam, and he started looking for gunfire from the tree lines before reality caught up to him. He was in a Beaver, not a Huey. He dropped down low and lowered his flaps to fly as slowly as possible over the lake, examining the surface to see if he thought it safe to land. He saw a small area of open water at the far end of the lake. "I'm sorry. I don't think I can get in there. I might try it close to shore if I was by myself, but I can't do it with all of you in here with me." He pulled up and started to circle over the lodge when Lizzie came running out the door.

"Elizabeth! That's my Elizabeth!" Charles was pressing his face against the side window, trying to get a better view.

"I'm sorry, but I can't land," Dan said. "It just isn't safe!" He looked over at Sarah, who was sitting in the right front seat. "Grab that flashlight out of the storage compartment there, and take out a battery. James, write them a note and tell them we will be back in a couple of days when we can get it in. We'll go to Caribou, and tomorrow or the next day I'll come back by myself when it's safer and pick them up."

James started writing the note, disappointment written all over his face.

Charles interrupted him as James was writing. "Wait a minute, James. What about the meadow about two miles north of the lodge? We've got skis on. We don't need to land on the lake."

"I don't know. Do you think we can get back out again? How much room do you need, Dan?"

"I can get it out in eleven hundred feet if I have to. I'd like a little more room though for comfort."

"Let's go take a look, James," said Charles. "Then we can tell Jed what we're doing."

Dan waggled the wings a couple of times and then turned the plane north. Moments later, they overflew the meadow Charles was talking about.

"It's long enough, but I want to take a good look to be sure there aren't any obstructions we can't see from up here." Dan lowered the flaps and cut power as low as he could and still stay in the air as he flew the length of the meadow, then turned and flew back the other direction. "Looks okay. Write 'meadow two miles north' and put it in the flashlight. Tie this streamer to it, and we'll drop it to Jed as we fly back over."

CHAPTER 90

Lizzie wailed in disappointment when the plane turned north and flew out of sight, but Jed was more taciturn. He recognized that the plane's appearance and circling overhead meant they had been found, and help was coming. He didn't think the ice was safe to land on yet. They were going somewhere to land but would be back in a few days. The sound of the engine didn't totally die out though, and in a few minutes he heard it approaching, and once again it circled around the lodge. When the plane flew directly over them, he saw something silver with a long streamer behind it dropping from the passenger window. It came to rest buried in the snow down by the lake. Fortunately, the streamer was yellow and not white, or they never would have found it. Lizzie started floundering through the snow to get it, but Jed told her to wait.

"I've got my snowshoes on, Lizzie. Let me get it." He trotted until he reached the end of the streamer. Hand over hand, he pulled it in until the flashlight appeared. He knocked the loose snow off and looked at it curiously, trying to decipher why they would drop a flashlight.

Lizzie had gotten there by then anyway. "Maybe there's something in it."

Shaking his head at his slow thinking, Jed unscrewed the end to find the note. "It says 'meadow two miles north'! They are going to land! Let's get you some snowshoes. You'll never make it without them."

CHAPTER 91

Dan Hixon flew low and slow over the meadow once again looking carefully for any hidden obstructions but didn't see any. He flew over again from the other direction, this time turning on his landing lights to see if there was anything to be seen in the gathering gloom. He and Sarah looked carefully and saw nothing that should be a problem.

"Okay, everyone. Be sure your seat belts are snug."

Those behind the second row couldn't hear him, so the word was passed back. Dan brought the plane in to land and flared just before touching down on the powdery surface. Snow billowed in their wake as he chopped power, and they felt the plane slowing quickly.

The rock wasn't very big, and the snow covered it completely. Six inches to one side or the other and they would have missed it. The right ski struck the top of the rock, and it was enough to cause the plane to lurch and turn abruptly to the right. The plane settled and didn't tip as it slid to a stop just before the trees. Quickly, Dan killed the engine and shut off the fuel, just in case.

"Everybody okay?" he shouted to those in the back.

Everyone looked at the others, shaken by the experience, but no one was hurt.

"Okay. Everyone stay where you are for the moment. James, Charles, want to hand me my coat, and grab yours? We have to be certain the plane is all right."

The men clambered from the plane, quickly closing the doors to retain the heat. It didn't take long to see the damage. The tip of the ski was bent up and back, with a crack splitting it from the front halfway back. After a rapid but careful inspection, Dan determined there was no damage to the strut or anything else. The only loss was the ski.

"Now I remember why I quit bush flying," Dan mumbled. "It doesn't take much to get you in trouble out here. It's a good thing we had slowed so much."

"Nobody's hurt. Things could be a lot worse. What do we do now?" asked Charles.

"I'm going to get on the radio and see if I can raise anyone at Caribou or someone flying nearby," Dan said. "You know, this is my fault. I should have waited for Jed to get out here and walk the area to be sure there wasn't anything here, but I was afraid of losing the light. It's going to get dark before long."

James put his hand on Dan's shoulder. "Look, Dan, I would have done the same thing, except I probably would have just flown over once and put it down. I could have said to wait a bit, but I didn't. Jed probably wouldn't have seen the rock anyway. Don't blame yourself. We aren't in bad shape. There is plenty of room in the lodge, and we'll get hold of someone. I'll have them call Dave at Fisheries, and he'll have another ski dropped to us."

"Okay, folks, we hit a hidden rock and bent a ski," James said as he re-entered the plane. "Gather your gear together. We're going to spend the night at the lodge, but it isn't too far away, and we'll be fine there.

It will be cold, but we can make it a couple of miles. Unfortunately, we can't taxi to the end of the meadow, but we'll be fine. Jim, would you gather all the food we brought along? I don't know how much food Jed has on hand. We may need to supplement what he has."

Charles said, "Knowing him, I'm sure he has plenty laid aside for the winter. That lad is resourceful and not afraid to work. I don't know of anyone I'd rather have my Elizabeth stranded with if I had to choose. We'll probably eat better than at home."

Mary, who had been silent nearly the entire trip, hugged Charles. "Thanks, Charles. That was sweet."

"Sweet, nothing! I've always hoped Jed and Elizabeth would notice each other, but they never seemed to."

After repeated tries, Dan Hixon was unable to reach anyone at Caribou Approach. "We're down too low to get them, boss. Most bush pilots monitor the emergency channel. I'll try it next."

After several attempts on the emergency channel, Dan was able to raise another pilot, although faintly. It took repeated transmissions before he was able to communicate, and the other pilot told him to stand by; he was flying their direction and would call back in a few minutes.

Charles helped the ladies step down from the plane and steadied them in the snow until they got their bearings. Sitting in somewhat cramped conditions and then trying to stand on the slippery surface was difficult at first. The ice under the snow made it treacherous. Sue gave Charles a one-armed hug and whispered in his ear, "Honey, you are getting your daughter back. I'm so excited!"

Charles hugged her back. "Me, too! I want to thank you. I don't know if I would have made it had you not been there for me. You will love her, and I know she will love you."

CHAPTER 92

Jed broke the trail for Lizzie going through the woods toward the meadow. Tommy trotted along beside her. Lizzie kept trying to hurry Jed, but he told her to be patient.

"If you hurry too fast, you will sweat, and then the sweat can freeze against your skin. Maybe not so much in this weather, but still it will chill you when you need the heat."

It took them a little over forty-five minutes to make the trek after Lizzie got snowshoes. At last, they emerged from the tree line and saw the plane at the far end of the meadow. Lizzie let out a squeal of joy and broke into a stumbling run on her snowshoes for the plane. Tommy stayed right at her side.

Charles saw a bearded man break out of the trees and then saw Lizzie behind him. He tried running toward her but slipped and fell on the ice before getting very far. He jumped up, unhurt, and hurried with more caution. James and Mary saw Charles start running and followed closely behind him, with James steadying Mary. It was a tearful yet joyful reunion in the middle of the meadow when they reached each other. Charles hugged Elizabeth tightly as they made their way back to the plane. She had to reassure Tommy it was okay. He kept trying to get between them and growled at Charles more than once. Sue and Jimmy walked out to meet them.

"Elizabeth, I want you to meet some very special people. This is Sue Jenson and her son, Jim. Sue is a nurse who cared for me when I was in the hospital."

"Oh, no, Daddy! Are you okay?"

"Oh, I'm fine now. Just stress. But Sue has been taking care of me ever since. I hope you like her because she means a lot to me, and I've asked her to marry me. I know it is kind of quick to spring it on you, but . . ." he paused as Lizzie jumped over to Sue and embraced her, squealing with joy.

"I'm so happy! I've been wanting him to find someone to care for! You are the answer to my prayers."

Sue hugged her back, happy to be accepted so readily.

"And I get a brother, too!" Jimmy was not quite as enthusiastic about the hug he received but was gracious enough to endure it. He still wasn't quite to the point of caring for hugs from girls.

Jed wrapped his arms around James and Mary at the same time and squeezed. He was so happy to finally be found.

Finally, James broke away from the embrace and wiped his eyes. "What happened, son? Wait, before you tell me about it." He waved Sarah over and said, "This is Detective Summers. She has been looking for you all this time. She needs to hear this, too."

Charles, Sue, and Jimmy also huddled around to listen as Jed told the story. "When we got back to the school, I got the message to take Lizzie home. Pete was waiting for us just outside of the school driveway, pretending to be broken down. When I drove him to the airport, he pulled a gun on Lizzie and me and made us get in the plane, and he brought us here. He said he was going to someplace in the Caribbean, that he needed money for gambling debts, and that you wouldn't loan it to him."

Both James and Detective Summers nodded their heads.

"He told me there were enough supplies for the fishing trip to take care of us until you sent him the ransom, and then he would tell you where to find us. He said he didn't want to hurt us, but he was afraid for his life. Pete broke the short-wave radio, so I couldn't call out for help. He started to take off in the plane, but he hit a goose right after lifting off, dragged a wingtip, and crashed. I couldn't get out there before the plane sank, though I did salvage one of the floats. We've been getting along okay, but we sure are glad to see you!"

Detective Summers put out her hand and said, "I think you did very well. You can be proud of yourself, young man. One question for you, though. What did he do for fuel? I know a Beaver doesn't have the range to get here."

"Pete had several drums of gasoline on board. He landed on a small lake partway here and pumped the gas into the tanks from the barrels. He had enough to get him partway down the coast to the Caribbean, too. He said he would be far enough away that you would never be able to figure out where he went."

Detective Summers nodded. "Just what Dan guessed. I'm so relieved to be able to pull your case out of the cold case files and put it in the closed case files."

Dan Hixon walked over from the airplane. "I finally got hold of Dave at Fisheries through a relay from another pilot. I used your name, and he is going to have a civilian bush pilot fly another ski up here tomorrow. I just have to mark the rock we hit so he can avoid it. I'll also walk the meadow first to be sure there aren't any other obstacles. If I hadn't been in such a hurry, I would have had Jed walk it for me and flown in tomorrow. Would have been a lot smarter all around; we could have been badly hurt."

"I don't think we would have let you wait," James said. "We really wanted to get in here. Like I said, Jed probably wouldn't have seen that rock anyway. You don't have need to blame yourself."

"Okay, boss. If you say so, but next time I'll be smarter."

CHAPTER 93

Supper was over, and everyone was seated on couches around the fireplace getting reacquainted, or acquainted as the case might be, except for Jim. He lay with Tommy on the bearskin rug on the floor. He kept stroking the fur and luxuriating in its softness. He also admired the buckskins both Jed and Lizzie were wearing. He asked Jed where he had gotten them, and his respect for Jed went way up when Jed told him he had made them, as well as the moccasins he wore. Jim asked if he would make him a set as well, but Charles said, "No, if you want some, you have to make them yourself." He winked. "Perhaps you can make them after you get your own deer next fall."

Jim's grin threatened to split his face.

Before everyone went to bed, Jed asked Charles to step outside for just a minute; he needed to speak with him privately.

Charles had a knowing look in his eye as he stood, and they walked out the door together. A number of thoughts flashed through Charles's mind. He thought of Collette and how sorry he was she could not be here for what he knew was coming. The torment of Elizabeth's disappearance and all that had transpired in the last nine months of wondering and searching was on his mind. He thought of Sue and how Sue had come into his life as a result of his panic attack, bringing with her a new son for him to love and raise. Charles knew he would lose his daughter again, but this loss was one he was more than happy to accept.

"Sir, I would like your permission to marry your daughter. I understand how it looks, with us up here alone. But I assure you we have behaved properly, and I have treated her with honor and respect." Jed took a deep breath. "I love Lizzie, and I will always care for her."

Charles reached out with one arm and gathered Jed to him in a gentle hug. "I know, son. I can see how you've cared for Elizabeth, and I know from her actions that you have respected her." Tears pooled in Charles's eyes, and he paused for a deep breath. "I want you to know I appreciate the way you respected and cared for her, and if her mother was here, I know she would as well. Although I hate to lose Elizabeth again, I'll agree on one condition."

Charles paused, and Jed looked at him, perplexed.

"It must be a double wedding."